THE L

Series Titles

Hoist House: A Novella & Stories
Jenny Robertson

Self-Defense
Corey Mertes

Where Are Your People From?
James B. De Monte

Finding the Bones: Stories & A Novella
Nikki Kallio

Sometimes Creek
Steve Fox

The Plagues
Joe Baumann

The Clayfields
Elise Gregory

Kind of Blue
Christopher Chambers

Evangelina Everyday
Dawn Burns

Township
Jamie Lyn Smith

Responsible Adults
Patricia Ann McNair

Great Escapes from Detroit
Joseph O'Malley

Nothing to Lose
Kim Suhr

The Appointed Hour
Susanne Davis

The author and her mother.

Praise for
Hoist House: A Novella & Stories

"Thank you, Jenny Robertson for these ecstatic explorations of our dark Midwestern hearts: the paranoiacs, the criminals, small town kids yearning for trouble, and for good measure, the romantic betrayal of a circus clown. These comedies and tragedies are sweaty and fragrant, brimming with energy, and the language is exuberant, whether in the bar with Toad Bear, night skating with the family on thin ice, or going deep into the mines. And all through these stories, sex simmers just below the surface."

—Bonnie Jo Campbell
National Book Award Finalist
author of *American Salvage* and *Mothers, Tell Your Daughters*

"The stories of *Hoist House* open on strikingly different scenes with a unique and varied cast of characters—a dominatrix, a storm chaser, a trio of middle-aged friends, a Finnish family settled in a Minnesota mining town—but all their lives are constrained, on the verge of caving in, of toppling over. Flawed and gorgeous, they all struggle to emerge. Robertson is so in tune with their wants, needs, and fears as individuals, but also how each character plays against each other in the dynamics of a small town, a family, a friend group, or a couple. Beautiful and shattering, these stories cut deep grooves into my memory, and in the end, I'm left with young Sadie's flush-faced feeling of skating on new ice: 'As if we were given just what we needed to survive and could find joy in the heat inside of us.'"

—Alexandra Lytton Regalado
author of *Relinquenda*

"I flat-out love this book. Jenny Robertson's stories evoke my favorite Midwestern writers: Jon Hassler, Joan Chase, and Jim Harrison—no-nonsense storytellers who lure you in with a sentence and then keep you rapt with prose as straight as an arrow aimed at your heart. *Hoist House* is everything you could possibly want in a debut."

—John McNally
author of *The Fear of Everything* and *The Book of Ralph*

"Jenny Robertson's *Hoist House* is beautifully written, a convergence of whimsy and pathos that channels poignantly the complex inner lives of her compassionately rendered characters, still on the prowl 'when all daylight creatures should be sleeping.' Wide awake and right there with them, I read this collection from cover to cover in a single sitting, marveling at its dazzle and dance, how every next story took me deeper, and deeper into that human realm where hilarity and tears combine in a rare and lovely kind of magic."

—Jack Driscoll
author of *Twenty Stories: New & Selected*

"Jenny Robertson's *Hoist House* will thrill readers with an exciting new voice. In her stories, readers will discover a style that breathes the air of the Great Lakes Upper Midwest, from the sharp winds of high lakes in northern Minnesota to the alcohol-stunned air of a Minneapolis bar in a swelter. Her stories shine with a concision that is a lighthouse beam through the darkness of our human states, but in none so accurately as 'Hoist House' (the novella), a stunning historical rendering of a Finnish immigrant family living the hard-core mining life of the Iron Range—a rare and accurate depiction of humanity on the edge, of people growing up marginal and beautiful and earth-cut by ore. It's a powerhouse of a read."

—Anne-Marie Oomen
author of *As Long As I Know You*

"*Hoist House* is an unforgettable collection of stories, a gritty and glittering panorama as graceful as it is riotously alive. Like the titular novella's Finnish immigrants descending the Minnesota mineshafts a century ago, Jenny Robertson's talents—the wit and elegance of her vision, and the sheer propulsive energy of her language—dig deep to excavate the vibrant souls of her characters and the outlandish American desire to break free and belong, all at once."

—Chris McCormick
author of *The Gimmicks* and *Desert Boys*

"Jenny Robertson's *Hoist House* is a study in the magic that can be discovered in the small spaces of the short story and the novella. Lives are lived, obsessions are exposed, histories (brief and extensive) are created and recreated. This fierce and fearless collection—set in a vividly drawn Midwestern landscape—is full of dangers and delights, intense voices and complex characters, unlikely allies and heroes. I did not want these stories to end. But they did, and beautifully so."

—Patricia Ann McNair
author of *Responsible Adults*

"Jenny Robertson's *Hoist House* mines the strata of its characters' lives alongside the emotional archaeology of the Upper Midwest. The stories and novella are grounded by loss and a hope for redemption—whether that finds its form in celebrations of the physical body or protection from the weathers of our world. Robertson's prose is perfectly suited to its forms. The vignettes are sharp and subtle, the stories sculpted with the bas-relief of physical geography. *Hoist House* explores political and psychological history in the way that the best fiction accomplishes its goals—her prose reflects its immigrant characters as they move into the complications of our modern landscapes."

—Elizabeth Oness
author of *Twelve Rivers of the Body* and *Fallibility*

"*Hoist House* amazes me with its unforgettable cast of characters, like Finnish people tied to a dangerous Minnesota iron mine during the early Twentieth Century in the title novella. Sadie, the wonderful young narrator, provides acute observations and details while coming of age and discovering her place in a community where most other women are hampered by daily work at home. This unique tale includes lechers, thieves, moonshiners, and slackers as well as many decent folks. Jenny Robertson has conjured a stunning debut that every reader should cherish."

—Craig Lesley
author of *Winterkill* and *The Sky Fisherman*

Hoist House

A Novella & Stories

Jenny Robertson

Cornerstone Press
Stevens Point, Wisconsin

Cornerstone Press, Stevens Point, Wisconsin 54481
Copyright © 2023 Jenny Robertson
www.uwsp.edu/cornerstone

Printed in the United States of America by
Point Print and Design Studio, Stevens Point, Wisconsin

Library of Congress Control Number: 2022949223
ISBN: 979-8-9869663-5-9

All rights reserved.

This is a work of fiction. Names, characters, businesses, places, events, and incidents are either the products of the author's imagination or used in a fictitious manner. Any resemblance to actual persons, living or dead, or actual events is purely coincidental.

Cover art: "Sunset on Lake Ore-be-gone, as seen from the Sherwood Forest Campground in Gilbert, Minnesota" © Tony Webster. This artwork is licensed under the Creative Commons Attribution-Share Alike 2.0 Generic license (https://creativecommons.org/licenses/by-sa/2.0/deed.en). No changes were made to the original artwork.

Cornerstone Press titles are produced in courses and internships offered by the Department of English at the University of Wisconsin–Stevens Point.

DIRECTOR & PUBLISHER EXECUTIVE EDITOR
Dr. Ross K. Tangedal   Jeff Snowbarger

SENIOR EDITORS
Lexie Neeley, Monica Swinick, Kala Buttke

PRESS STAFF
Ellie Atkinson, Lauren Engelbreth, Hannah Fenrick, Patrick Fogarty, Angela Green, Cal Henkens, Brett Hill, Julia Kaufman, Catriona Scheinost, Maria Scherer, Cash Van Stiphout, Matt Vancik, Abbi Wasielewski

*To my beloved kiddo,
bright and brave in the face of an imperfect world*

Also by Jenny Robertson:

Hard Winter, First Thaw

Contents

Sex-O-Rama, 1993 • 1

Lifted • 17

The Triumphant Return of Maggie Pancake • 19

Risen • 35

Ground Truth • 37

The Improviser • 53

Hoist House • 55

Acknowledgments • 187

Sex-O-Rama, 1993

Cher Bebe was supposed to be a dentist. Or a minister. His parents couldn't agree, so they kept both possibilities in mind as he grew older and taller, his body flowering far above them, his mouth sassier, his grades falling farther each year, his pants tighter, the color of his shirts pineapple, grape, cherry, lime and orange, painted to his torso so he looked more and more like a bird. But not like Admiral, the small grey cockatiel they'd kept in a rectangle cage in the corner of the living room. So sad it pulled out its feathers, so disturbed it made love to a girl bird made from a balled up and twisted tube sock then squawked in frustration to an empty room.

* * *

Cher Bebe emerged from the dressing room at eight o'clock, ready for this week's Sex-O-Rama. He wore his grandfather's Mardi Gras headdress, a fifteen-pound wedding cake of linked beads, rainbow-dyed pelican feathers, and punctured cockle shells which had arrived at his Minneapolis doorstep the previous year. He wore size fifteen thigh-high lace-up black leather boots and a loincloth sewn from Tibetan peace flags. In a shoulder holster, he carried a slim whip. Four states to the south, his father was dying. Steve, his boss, had descended from his record-lined office, perpetually redolent of grass and tequila, and stood on the empty dancefloor, shouting.

Sex O Rama, 1993

"Who was fucking responsible for cleaning last night?" Steve pressed a hairy hand into a smear of mud left over from Wednesday's Ladies' Wrestling and shook it in the air. "I pay you, don't I? Don't I? Somebody fucking fix this right now, or you're all fired."

Bartenders left their limes mid-prep. DJ Spinlove left his strobes. The bouncers left their mirrors, and all of First Avenue's employees knelt on the ground with rags and wet sponges until the floor was clean. Except Cher Bebe. He didn't kneel for anyone, not even if they paid. Not since his last year of high school, when his band director, in an effort to "harden him up," unzipped his corduroys and presented his syllabus.

Cher Bebe stayed in the shadows until Steve huffed up the stairs to the balcony, slammed his office door, and everyone returned to their usual positions. He found Melanie behind the bar.

"Honey, set me up. Double kamikaze."

"Go easy on the sinners tonight," she said. "No scars."

"Love, you know I only scar the ones who need it." He returned the empty shot glass. "If my mother calls, flash me."

"Something going on?"

"Just do it. Please."

Melanie shrugged her substantial shoulders. "Fine. Purple light means call your mother." When the club was busy, they couldn't hear each other, so they used industrial glowsticks as signals, like airport runway marshals guiding a plane. White meant refill toilet paper. Yellow meant mop up piss or puke. Blue was for O.D. Red for fight. The speed of the flash signaled the intensity of the problem, and the closest hands were expected to respond. The purple light was extra, for personal communications.

Melanie leaned back and yelled through cupped and hennaed hands. "Hey! My purple is for Sha tonight." Lights flashed back in response from all directions, trippy fireflies. He'd given up on correcting their pronunciation of his chosen name. No one here could wrap their tongues around it. Cher, pronounced "share", was all they could manage. He told them Sha, like "shaw", and pictured his grandmother's voice. *Cher Bebe,* her mouth forming the last two syllables on the exhale, soft as an infant's: *bay bay.*

The name was a mantra, a soft fall of love. Claim what you're called and they can't touch you. Cover yourself in a costume so bright and imposing you dazzle. Lights, action. No one can look past you, but they can't see into you either.

At nine o'clock the doors opened, admitting an assortment of Twin Cities freaks, addicts, and voyeurs. Busty young women who peeled off long winter coats to reveal string bikinis were let in free, served strong drinks, and directed to the hot tub onstage. Frat boys arrived in packs and were charged extra. Older, married, and anti-social people took their beers up to the balcony and those who had come to be seen—pretty boys, tough girls, and everyone in between—clogged the bars and commandeered the dance floor.

Cher Bebe waited for his cue, the opening beats of Salt-N-Pepa—*ah, push it*—and strode onto the stage. The hot tub girls squealed, threw their bare legs out of the water and, dripping, surrounded him. They stroked his oiled chest, rubbed against his loincloth, and pushed it every Midwestern way they knew how. After a particularly brazen nymph reached on tiptoes for his headdress, Cher Bebe showed her the whip and marched into the crowd, looking for someone who wasn't dancing. *Now wait a minute, y'all, this dance ain't for everybody, only the sexy people.*

He found the night's victims easily. Eggheads, a group of college kids who had shown up as a joke, to watch but not play. This type often took notes, maybe hoping to write a sociology paper: *Nocturnal Observations at Sex-O-Rama: A Case Study.*

Three boys and a girl, each pale as January. The college boys stared at the dancers, traded smart remarks and snickered, but the lone girl was collapsing upon herself like a dying star. Her posture spoke of long nights with hardcovers and hot tea. But all four sat up straight when they realized Cher Bebe was aimed at their table. "IDs," he said. "Now."

The bookish redhead handed hers over, moon-eyed. "They checked us at the door."

"Yes, *ma'am*," he said. "Thank you."

The boy next to her rummaged in his khakis. "Fuck. Just a minute."

They were a couple, Cher Bebe realized, watching her watch her helpless boyfriend, who still couldn't find his card. Probably they had a little sex. Maybe even a lot. Probably they tried sixty-nine because they'd seen it in a book, each so intent on earning an A for effort they never felt the other's tongue.

"Here," Khaki Side-part said, and handed Cher Bebe his ID as though it were a well-polished curriculum vitae.

"*Merci beaucoup.*" Cher Bebe tucked the four fake IDs into a secret pocket in his peace flags. "Darlings," he extended a hand to the boy and girl, "come with me."

Cher Bebe pulled the young lovers onto the stage, which was now awash with tub water and slippery people. He brought them to the edge, in front of everyone, and pressed them together as though he were a child marrying Barbie and Ken. "Show us your moves," he cooed into their delicate pink ears.

"I don't know," she said, but the boyfriend leaned in for a kiss. For a long ten seconds, they did their best. The boy tried to find his rhythm and the girl closed her eyes. People hooted and clapped, if only to honor the bravery and awkwardness on display. Then the boy shoved his hands up her shirt, popped her buttons free, and she slapped him, in tears.

When Cher Bebe saw she was going to bolt, he separated them. "Stay here," he told her. "Watch this."

Can't you hear the music's pumpin' hard like I wish you would? Now push it.

In one quick move Cher Bebe untucked the boyfriend's shirt from his khakis. A trio of bikini girls stepped in to finish the work. Before Salt-N-Pepa stopped spinning, the boy was in the hot tub in his plaid flannel boxers, and the girl had fled the stage.

* * *

Purple light shone from Melanie's station. Cher Bebe whipped a clear path to the bar, turned off the strobe, and entered one of the dozen wooden phone booths that lined the back wall. They were commonly used for meetings—their swinging doors afforded some privacy and the cubicles themselves could hold two friendly people—but the phones worked too and local calls were free.

The bench inside the oiled oak booth felt almost like a church pew. At first, his mother's voice made no impact, but Cher Bebe heard her the second time she spoke his name.

"John."

"I'm here. How's he doing?"

"Not long now. He's comfortable."

"That's good."

"He's going to want to hear your voice."

"You think he can hear me?"

"Yes."

"Call me when it's almost over. I'll do it then."

"Not now?"

"No. Not yet."

"All right. I'll call when it's time."

Though he knew his father was now a shriveled husk of his former self, lying on a hospice bed in the sitting room, Cher Bebe still pictured him full-sized, in his practice, Decoudreau Dentistry, the steel implements forever laid out on a fresh sheet of blue paper. Even with that divider, Cher Bebe could feel the potential of metal against metal: quiet, forbidding, and serious, awaiting the next sinner. He was the confessor and judge and it didn't matter what you told him, he could see all when he asked you to say *ahh*. Coffee, sugar, cigarettes, junk food, alcohol, lack of brushing, lack of flossing. All your secret sins revealed, all your lapses in character. While his mother wanted him to be a supplicant to Jesus, to sing and confess and praise and, eventually, to minister, his father wanted him on the side of the archangels, the heavy hand and clear eye of judgment. Fix the fallen, curb their wanton ways, put the fear of God, in your own form, into their weak flesh. There was a narrow way, and a dentist pointed people to it.

Cher Bebe didn't know what you said to a dying father, one you hadn't spoken to in years.

* * *

For ten bucks a pop, Cher Bebe would paddle your backside. Fifteen without pants. Twenty for a soft whipping. A fifty got you flogged. After the phone call, he made one-twenty in less than an hour upstairs, mostly regulars who couldn't care less about tonight's hot tub and club music, who just needed a fix. Sometimes the customers talked. Often they cried. The ones who scared him laughed, louder and more joyfully the harder he hit.

There was a gun range in the basement—who knew why—another way for Steve to crazy up the place. Usually, everything down there went fine. Even though all the shooters were drunk and high, they had decorum, and somehow no one got shot. The closest they got was two years ago when this kid showed up far past loaded, dressed in a camo hoodie, Carhartts and muck boots, carrying a .22. He was shaking cold and soaking wet, and screamed over and over that he'd sinned and needed to be punished.

The gun enthusiasts didn't want to argue with him in that state, and no one wanted to shoot him. But the police weren't exactly welcome either, so someone ran to get Cher Bebe.

The kid stopped yelling when he entered the room. He had maybe never been that close to a six-foot-three Creole man wearing a red glitter G-string. He held his gun close to his chest and stared at Cher Bebe, crying.

"Put it down."

The kid shook his head.

Cher Bebe drew his whip. "How can I punish you while you're carrying that thing? What if it goes off, hurts somebody?"

That set the kid off even more. He was snotting everywhere, but he put the gun down. Two men ran in like Wimbledon ball-boys and scooped it from the floor.

"Do you need a public confession?"

"What?"

"Do you want to confess your sins in front of these people?"

Without his gun, the kid was a pitiful sight. Thin and grimy, drunk and sad. He seemed unable to find the will to speak.

"Out," Cher Bebe said. "Everybody."

When they were alone, Cher Bebe said, "Tell me everything, and I will redeem you. Take off your jacket."

* * *

His last job upstairs was a light paddling for a couple dressed as Batman and Robin. They yelled "Pow!" and "Bam!" every time a blow landed and afterwards tipped him an extra twenty bucks.

Hands caressed him from all sides as he descended the stairs. Most were gentle, but one greedy, grabby person required a quick knock on the head. Cher Bebe slid behind Melanie's bar and squeezed her shoulders. "You need anything?"

"Wash."

He scrubbed and rinsed two dozen glasses, then mixed himself another kamikaze.

"Hey Shawnee! Hey Red Lake! You Winnebago? Anishinaabe? Drinking on the job? When you gonna give me my headdress back?" The man yelling from the other side of the bar wore his usual green jacket, whose patches marked him as U.S. Air Force, Vietnam Veteran.

"Hey George."

"Hey beautiful abomination. I'm serious about the headdress. You can't keep it."

Cher Bebe laughed. "Tell that to my grandmother. She made it."

"Nah," George said. "My grandmother dropped it in the stream at Itasca and it floated down the Mississippi to your grandmother's house. She hosed it off and claimed it as her own." He shook his head. "It's how you got all those Mardi Gras Indians, from my family. We're the droppingest motherfuckers you ever met, lose all kinds of shit, all the time."

"You going to dance tonight?"

"Nah, I like this seat." George twirled his barstool back and forth. "I can see everything from here. Like that." He pointed up to the mezzanine.

Steve had coked himself up to the point of pure madness. He was hanging upside down from the railing by his knees, like a fourth-grader ready for a cherry drop.

Though the boss preferred concert nights over money-makers like Sex-O-Rama, he must have heard the DJ play "Whoomp! (there it is)" and wanted to be present for the lines: *and my man Steve roll'n, bring it back ya'll bring it back.* Steve's entourage let him ride out the song in bat position, then pulled him to safety.

The shot would do a little to blunt the edges, but not enough. Steve was occupied, so Cher Bebe took a break in the Subhuman room, a dark pit hidden under a trapdoor backstage.

"Sha."

"Who's that? Casey?"

"Yeah, me and Mike." A joint appeared from a soft pile of blankets and coats.

"Thanks, sugar. Needed that." Cher Bebe's boots touched something soft. "Who else is in here?"

"Tony and some girl."

"Give me a light."

Tony Moretti, one of the set-up guys, had obviously clocked out for the night. He was fully occupied with the girl beneath him, visible only as a bare belly and a cloud of red hair.

That hair. Cher Bebe leaned in closer with the lighter. "Aw, shit."

"What?"

"Tony, get the fuck up."

Tony untangled his tongue long enough to tell him to screw off.

Cher Bebe pushed his bootheel in Tony's ass until he rolled over.

"You! You're evil." The bookish girl slurred her words and stank of sangria.

"Yes, honey, I'm a bad man. But I'm your only hope."

Casey and Mike held the trap door open so Cher Bebe could drag the girl from the pit. The purple light was back on.

He stuffed the girl in one phone booth and himself in another.

"Hello."

His mother's breath was fast but shallow, her voice soft. "He's close now."

He thought he heard a catch, an almost sob, but knew she wouldn't permit it until everything was done.

"John," she said. "John, I'm putting the phone to his ear now. Only he can hear you. Please say what you need to say."

* * *

Cher Bebe worshipped his own arms, his long legs, worshipped the flat expanse of his stomach. He oiled his smooth skin, praised the light that rode his muscles' curves. His warm hand acknowledged the perfection of the whole of him. Stayed in contact with that goodness.

His father, Dr. Decoudreau, never showed his bare torso, though it pressed hard against the fabric of his button-down shirts. He fed his body secret extra meals, second breakfasts on the way into the office he'd built in his old neighborhood, the 7th Ward, far from their home in Metairie. Long lunches in the mini-malls: crab wontons, shrimp alfredo, biscuits and white gravy, sausage and eggs. His console was stuffed with receipts from China Palace, Willie Mae's Scotch House, Chick-fil-A. Cher Bebe used to look through them when he waited for his father to complete an errand and wondered why he didn't throw away the evidence of his vice. Some sort of guilt? Or was it just more of his father's need to keep track, to control by adding the numbers up, marking the dates. Raising up his desire to eat these meals from mere gluttony, lust, and need into the real world of accounts.

He could tell his father he was eating well. That he was cooking his mother's recipes. He could share memories of her dancing in the kitchen, singing along to Art Neville: *I've got it bad, it's alright.* Tell the good doctor he could picture her at a dance, enjoying herself, and imagine how the two of them, who were so different, came to be. How he came to be. His father would have been dressed in a suit and tie, slim and serious then—he'd seen the pictures—long arms and legs, no padding, though Cher Bebe knew he already had that large appetite. That never-filled feeling. His mother must have looked like everything he wanted, everything he wasn't: relaxed in body, confident in movement, attuned to melody and rhythm. Sure of her place, of her right to move.

Cher Bebe pictured him a kind of Frankenstein's monster, drawn to move one great foot after another toward her, pulled by her light, pulled by the swing of her hips. It was all destined, the matches that God ordained. He built deficiencies into each clay being: each one lacking something, each one hungry to take a little bit of what another one's got. He pictured his monster father, his incomplete clay figure father, taking his mother into his arms, stilling those hips with his own, chilling her and warming her with his silent need. Knowing his mother, she would have been curious. She would have understood that he needed her, that she fit him, and from there, with God's blessing, they'd make him from the clay.

* * *

He took the girl into his dressing room, said, "Love, do you want to go home?"

She shook her head no, and made a pillow out of his street clothes, which were lying on the vinyl loveseat in the corner. "I want to sleep."

"Can you trust any of your friends?"

"Leo," she said. "He's not an asshole."

"Which one's Leo?"

"Dark hair, skinny...dances like Michael Stipe."

* * *

"Where've you been?" Melanie shouted over the heads of Sex-O-Rama-crazed patrons.

"Working, honey, as always."

"Better get your ass onstage soon. Steve's been looking for you."

"Stay with the action!" Cher Bebe said, in his best Steve impression.

"Never leave the action!" Melanie agreed.

After downing one Patron, for juice, Cher Bebe stopped by Spinlove, requested "Cream" and went looking for Michael Stipe. He wasn't hard to find. Arms hanging stiff by his sides but unhinged at the shoulders so they swung back and forth like the chains of a park swing. Attempting a little style, bangs long enough to poke him in the eye. Long serious face pointed toward the ground. Hips that didn't know they were hips. Knees buckling, scarecrow, set the whole slim body in motion.

Not one to waste a good opportunity, Cher Bebe corralled the boy with his whip and gently pulled him near.

"Your friend," he whispered, "is drunk in my dressing room."

* * *

It was Prince's fault he was here at all. The way he straddled and fucked his guitar, his slim body poured into a velvet suit. The way he looked out from under fat lashes to smote sex into your heart. *Live, at First Avenue*, the TV said. *His club, Minneapolis, Minnesota.* He just walked in when he wanted to and said he was putting on a show. Cher Bebe bought a ticket on the *City of New Orleans* the day after graduation with the money the church ladies had given him through his mother, on the sly—even though he had fallen—in perfumed envelopes, crisp twenties they'd saved from their jobs. He didn't know how they managed to save so much for graduations, for birthdays, for the donation plate. Or maybe he did: scrimping on themselves, clothes on sale or second-hand, mending the rough-edged sheet, coupons and prayer, and work, work, work. Always work.

He put the good women's money toward a train ticket to sin. Got off a bus in Minneapolis in the middle of May, blossoms and green grass, high glass buildings and dirt on the sidewalks leading to First Avenue, just around the corner from the station. The outside of the building: white stars painted on black bricks. The names of all the people who'd played the stage written in bold and loopy cursive. It was late in the day, last heat of sun readying to dive down and be lost for the rest of the starless northern city night. A line of cool kids stalked the avenue, their hair teased up and held with spray, the girls in leather and fishnet, fake fur and ripped t-shirt. Boys in the same. Girls in jeans. Boys in jeans. Short hair. Long hair. A winding line, cigarettes. *You want some*, a short girl with a pink fade asked Cher Bebe, extending in her hand a crushed pack of Native Spirits. He didn't smoke, didn't need that kind of haze in his lungs, but he said *Sure. Yes I do.* And he stayed in line, paid ten dollars of church money to get in the door. Prince was not on stage. But Cher Bebe could see him even so, his echo loose above the worn boards, scratched but black as black. The sick high assault of a bent string, and the resulting wave, he heard just as clear as if he had been there when the artist played it.

He walked as a ghost through the building, silent in the midst of noise. He seemed to disappear. He seemed to come alive. Music low through the speakers, something about a Zamboni, in a twangy white boy voice. He heard his own voice in his ears, *you're needed here*, and he almost wept.

* * *

Cher Bebe sat in his dressing room, the glitter stars faintly glowing in the half-light. Bulbs burnt out, the way he preferred it. Soft light after all the noise. Off came the crown, all fifteen pounds of it. Even the feathers were tired. They hung down listless, their colors faded. You were only supposed to wear them for one season, but Cher Bebe thought here, far from Carnival, he could use its protection. He agreed with the Chief of Chiefs, Tootie Montana, that it was better "to fight with the needle and thread," with the prettiness of costumes, than to sacrifice the bodies of men. Cher Bebe didn't know if it was alive—the crown his father's father wore, masking Indian with the White Eagles, this tradition his father had dropped—but somehow it knew how to rejuvenate itself. By next week, the next time he'd have occasion to wear it, it would have puffed up, air between all the layers. They would positively swirl on their mannikin head in his bedroom, waiting for him.

To roll a headdress, you need a clear surface, long and flat. Cher Bebe used a table. Remember Boy Scouts. Remember sleepovers. Remember your first lessons with a sleeping bag. Start with the head. Roll tight, but not too tight. Keep it straight. Roll down toward the feet, tucking in stray feathers as you go. When you're done, you should have a tidy cylinder, one that will fit in an over-the-shoulder bag, the kind in which you put foldable chairs. Cher Bebe's bag was green.

His feet ached, but he felt light in his exhaustion, as he always did after a night performing. Once his make-up was Noxema'd off, he used a witch hazel cloth, disposable, to remove the last traces. Though he left the eyeliner. A surprise for whoever might look up close. His brows brushed, his hair run through with bright-nailed fingers, Cher Bebe counted the money in his loincloth. Not a bad evening. Respectable. Plus the tip from the drunk girl and her Stipe, a wet five dollars.

* * *

Outside the curved world of First Ave, after the *good nights* and settling of accounts, Cher Bebe was surprised to see a toad nestled up against the meeting of concrete and concrete, in the narrow land of dirt from which a few brave dandelions fought for light. Though not large, it was squat and fat. It had presence. An intricate set of markings covered its skin: gray diamond on his head, leaf lines and bark patterns down his back and limbs. In another environment he would have blended right in. Downtown Minneapolis at three in the morning, not so much. Where was his water? His food? How did he protect his camouflaged body from the feet and tires of the city?

Cher Bebe crouched down and sang to it soft: *say Mardi Gras comin' and we ready to die, say mama told me, 'fore you leave home, you a little bitty boy, but you carry it on.*

Lifted

On a summer evening when all that surrounded him should have been comforting—cricket chorus, bright moon, scent of pine and wildflowers—the man's thoughts beleaguered him, laid blame on him and judged him. He sat alone on his porch. No interloper's footfall disturbed the air. But still, the noise of condemnation rose so shrill and high in his mind he could not bear to sit one moment longer, and he stood and found his feet, and his feet found the stairs to the ground that the people on his father's side had owned for a hundred years.

The path he followed from the porch through the yard and into the forest could easily have been just as old. More sins than the ones he himself had committed traveled this path. That's what he told himself as he moved, steady and quiet, into the cover of pine. Birds rustled in the branches and lifted from their evening beds. He thought moonlight and heat kept them on edge too, kept their eyes open even in tiredness, kept them awake when all daylight creatures should be sleeping.

As he fell further from the light of the clearing, and the forest sheltered him in deep shadow, the man felt more at peace. Here, at least, he knew what he was doing, what he headed for. Five minutes more and he reached the tree fort he had built with his sister, who was gone and married now, raising boys who would make their own trouble soon enough. Here the siblings had played games he always won. Here their mother never came to check. The games ended when his sister grew old enough to refuse to play and fast enough to outrun him.

On the wooden platform of the fort, plastic figures: a unicorn, a Cinderella in removable clothes, doll cups and saucers, pretend food. All new. Not his. He moved the toys closer together, so the unicorn and Cinderella touched noses. Then he knocked them down.

Back on the path, continuing, he felt only excitement. The voices that bothered him on the porch stilled their tongues. After not very long he came to the edge of the forest where a little house sat, all its lights turned out for the night. He stayed in the shadow under the trees and watched the house for a long time, until his heartbeat slowed to an easy rhythm.

Behind that last window was a child. He had watched her sleep before, had stood close to her window and watched her breathe. Had wondered about her. The man knew that even though her eyes were closed, the child, like the evening birds, was sleeping restless. From his pocket he pulled out a small knife, which he used to lift out the window screen. He laid the screen gently on the ground and reminded himself to replace it, after.

The Triumphant Return of Maggie Pancake

Three girls walked into a bar in Lumbertown. It had been ten years since Maggie Johanssen, thirty-one, last lived in this town or opened this door, which was painted with one flashy silver word: *Buoy*. They'd always called it The Boy, and in college, when they were back in town on Christmas or summer break, they'd ask each other, *You want to hit The Boy tonight?* This sultry late-June evening was the first of Maggie's week-long visit home, and it was time to hit The Boy again.

Following close behind Maggie was Deb Cherniak. Deb, mother to a third-grader and a four-year-old, had taken forever to get ready. They'd had to wait in her living room with her husband and kids while she tromped around upstairs, audibly cursing. Finally, she came downstairs wearing a pair of dress pants and her least-faded red shirt and said, "Who's ready to go to a PTA meeting?" Her husband had smiled and said, "Don't have club clothes anymore, huh?" as though motherhood had been a cruel trick he'd played on her, one that had consequences she hadn't quite yet grasped.

Joanna Berkin brought up the rear, spun in place on her lady lawyer shoes while using her remote to secure her car. It beeped, one lone goose honk. "Good to go, my dears,"

The Triumphant Return of Maggie Pancake

Joanna said. "That's the last responsible thing we need to do tonight."

Inside the Buoy, the sunlight and all sense of the outside world disappeared. There were a few high windows scattered about, but years of cigarette smoke had given them a hazy sheen. Through them, the poplars and jack pines outside appeared unreal and wavy. Vertical knotty pine boards lined the walls, the tables close together and branded with the names of light beers. The bar itself was long and golden brown, with two dark-haired men leaning their elbows on its bumpered edge. The TV above the bar replayed past glories of Minnesota Golden Gophers hockey.

"Wild night we picked," Deb said.

The Buoy hadn't changed at all, though entering it at thirty-one, Maggie felt out of place. She remembered the old expectation and excitement, but just last month her fiancé, Roy, a student at the clown college in Baraboo, had dumped her for a classmate whose stage name was Sunshine Flappy-Pants, and now Maggie felt more exhausted than hopeful. She peeked around the corner at the stage and dance floor. Absolutely empty. "Maybe everybody left when we stopped coming," she said.

"Or maybe it's 6 o'clock on a Tuesday night," Joanna said. She dropped her purse on a table, said, "Order me a virgin margarita. I have to pee."

"Joanna always has to pee," Deb told Maggie. "Announces it like she's the first woman in the world to get pregnant." Maggie knew that although Deb's two young children wore her down on a daily basis, she wanted another. Though her husband Joe argued otherwise, which, she claimed, made her uterus cramp so much she had to console it, saying, "Don't worry, he'll change his mind."

Maggie walked to the bar and placed their order. While the bartender shook the virgin marg, pulled a Grain Belt for Maggie, and mixed a Long Island iced tea for Deb, the two guys lifted their heads and stared at her as though they were deer and she a forest intruder. Men did that a lot, Maggie thought, stopped their grazing and conversation to look at a woman, with no sense that it wasn't polite to stare at a stranger, especially at close range.

Her body shifted in response to their eyes. She sucked in her gut, rolled her shoulders back. Earlier tonight, in her old bedroom at her parents' house, which had been turned into a craft room and was filled with her mother's slightly creepy multi-colored velour teddy bears, she'd liked the idea of appearing hot, on the loose with her long-time friends.

"Don't you look beautiful?" her mother had said before Maggie left the house. "Dan, honey, look at our Maggie Pancake."

Her parents, high school sweethearts, believed the world was good and just, and their daughter a brilliant and lovely go-getter. In the face of their unrelenting optimism, Maggie never had the heart to share her disappointments with them. Kids in school had called her Maggie Pancake in honor of her non-existent chest, but to this day her dad believed she'd earned the moniker in a blueberry pancake eating contest. Three weeks ago, when she'd called off her wedding, she'd considered telling her parents that a batch of contaminated face paint had caused Roy to forget who she was. She'd imagined them shedding actual tears for poor Roy, and never once questioning her story. Instead, just this one time, she broke down and told them everything: the unnatural beauty of the clown named Sunshine; the way Roy's weekends were suddenly always booked with children's birthday parties; how she waited for the clown car to arrive at her door, later and later on Saturday nights, until one night it didn't come home at all.

After being jilted, Maggie knew she could use some positive attention, but there was something about these guys' eyes that didn't require her consent or participation. *I don't care what you think about my ass*, she thought. She stared back at them, her mouth set in the disapproving teacher look she'd cultivated over the past five years at Milwaukee's Grover Pond Elementary.

The two men laughed, said something under their breath, then raised their drinks to her. The big hairy one looked like a Toad. Or a Bear. A Toad-Bear, and the other, the dark-haired skinny one with the leer, a Mongoose. Not completely freakish, she supposed, not animal men. Ten years ago, they might have been the kind of boys she and Deb and Joanna—and Josie, too—would've rubbed up against on the crowded dance floor. Would've kissed after too many drinks, so tipsy they could barely stand, before they were pulled out the door by whichever bored cohort had drawn the DD straw.

But then again, ten years ago these men would've smiled at Maggie, and not relied on grim tractor beam stares to draw her in.

One New Year's Eve, when they were twenty-one, they'd gotten together in Duluth, where Joanna was living. The three of them and Josie. Once the drinks took hold, they'd charged out to the dance floor, seeing who could move the most outrageously to "Pour Some Sugar on Me." They had felt powerful that night, unbreakable, their friendship a protective spell.

But that New Year's Eve, no one picked Josie. And the rest of them, mesmerized by the undulations of guys' bodies, didn't notice until it was too late that Josie was sobbing alone in the bathroom.

"Am I that ugly?" she'd asked Maggie, her wet, blotchy face in the mirror bracketed on either side by perfectly made-up girls avidly applying more make-up. "Am I unlovable?"

In the middle of that room of stage-ready girls, Maggie held her best friend like a child, whispered *no, no, you're beautiful, they're idiots, just idiots* until Josie stopped shaking.

* * *

Here, several beer mirrors graced the Buoy's walls. Mirrors etched with leaping silver-sided pike, mouths open and exposing rows of sawteeth in their elongated jaws. And bar posters that featured a pack of blondes in tight half-top Vikings jerseys and cutoff jean shorts, white ermine earflap hats and matching Sorel boots. The models seemed to mock Maggie with their tacky perfection as they leaned over their snowmobiles, their long, tanned legs goosebump-free even though it was winter.

The bartender, Tammy Detterlau, younger sister to a classmate of theirs, was still rocking the claw bang that had been a rite of passage in northern Minnesota in 1989. A whole generation of girls had learned—with mousse and spray, perm and Pik—how to arrest a tsunami mid-crest over their foreheads, immovable until the next shower.

Tammy said, "You want anything to eat?"

"Mozzarella sticks," Maggie said.

In Milwaukee, after Roy had moved out, waving goodbye from his packed station wagon with one silently apologetic hand, she'd become inexplicably enraged by the flyers pinned to the co-op bulletin board: *Processed meat causes cancer. Inhumane milk causes cancer. Your negative emotions and spiritual stuntedness cause cancer.* If a person had walked into that co-op and said, "I have cancer," a hundred shoppers would have looked down their noses and thought, "No wonder. What did you do?" Maggie had wanted to start shouting about Josie, who'd, for one adolescent year, subsisted only on salads. Miss 400-Yard-Dash Champion. Miss Brown Rice. Instead, Maggie snubbed the co-op and started ordering in: egg rolls and pizza, gyros and cheeseburgers. At the school's employee party at the Bierstube she'd drunk beer from a glass boot and stuffed herself on kielbasa. Then she'd danced it up with Ed Moore, one of the third-grade teachers, who'd been flirting with her all year.

"Hope you like lime and salt, baby," Joanna said as she took a deep pull on her drink.

"Do you miss the tequila?" Maggie asked. Though she was in no hurry, she believed that, eventually, she would be a French kind of mom, sipping red wine under an arbor at lunch, for the iron. But Ed, the third-grade teacher, had toddler twins and a wife at home. He who would never in this earthly life take her to France.

"Tequila and I haven't been friends for a while," Joanna said.

"We're so lucky," Deb said, tearing up out of nowhere and touching Joanna's belly, though she'd always hated it when people did that to her. "To be able to go through this. Ooh! I felt a little jump."

"Because Josie can't," Maggie said, finishing Deb's thought. "She would've been such a great mom."

Joanna winced, removed Deb's hand from her belly. "Sorry. I've got gas," she said, and reached for a mozzarella stick. "Well, I'm going to be a mom whether I'm any good at it or not."

"You're going to be great," Maggie and Deb both said.

"And for sure I'm not going to stick around the house like you did, Deb," she said. "I'd go nuts."

"It's not for everybody," Deb said, although she had said a million times that putting babies in daycare set them back emotionally for the rest of their lives. And was no doubt responsible for a good part of this nation's sociopathology.

"What do you think Josie would be doing right now?" Maggie said.

"She'd have two kids, like me," Deb said.

"Naw. She didn't want to start as early as you," Joanna said. Deb had James when she was twenty-three. She'd been pregnant with him when Josie died, and had told Maggie she still wondered if all the crying she'd done that year made the boy the overly serious and sensitive kid that he was. An eight-year-old Cub Scout way too concerned about merit badges. Maybe she'd skewed his stress hormones in utero. She worried about that, too.

"She'd have been Superwoman," Maggie said, and they all nodded. "Sugar cookies and homemade costumes and straight A's."

"And she'd still hold down a great job."

"And they'd take vacations to national parks and never argue."

"And she'd keep it all in scrapbooks," Deb said, a notoriously passionate scrapbooker. She'd made one for each child, and she often called Maggie on nights when Joe and the kids were asleep, after she'd drunk lots of chardonnay and looked through all the pictures, weepy because her kids were never going to be so small again.

"Hey ladies." The Mongoose pulled up a chair between Deb and Maggie, and Maggie moved over out of politeness. "What are we up to tonight?"

We, Maggie thought. So slimy.

"*We* are old friends catching up," she said, the schoolteacher talking to the student, though still she found herself sitting straighter against the chair back so as not to minimize her boobs.

"Ooh, that's great," the Mongoose said. "You ladies from around here?"

Joanna stared at the guy, said, "I'm from Preglandia," and leaned back to display her swollen belly.

"Yeah, you probably shouldn't be at a bar," he said, then made a head-to-toe scan of Deb. "Why don't you girls come sit with us?"

"I don't think so," Joanna said.

"We're good," Maggie said. "Thanks anyway."

While they were sipping their second drinks, and before all the mozzarella sticks had been eaten, Tammy offered them another round.

"From the guys at the bar," she said.

Deb laughed. "Why not? They think we're hot mamas."

Tammy set down their drinks. "Here's to the moms."

"Yucch," Joanna said, and pushed away her third virgin margarita. "I'm sorry, baby says no more lime. Water when you get a chance, Hon."

Because Deb and Joanna kept her apprised of local gossip, Maggie knew that Tammy's youngest boy, born premature, had had health problems ever since. Her ex left town soon after the spaghetti supper the town had thrown to cover the boy's medical costs, and the children's grandmother watched them on the nights Tammy worked. "How's Tyler these days?" Deb asked.

"He's a terror," Tammy said. "The medicine's working too well—you can't slow him down now."

"Isn't that the truth," Deb said. She always tried to equate other children's behavior with that of her own, even when they had nothing in common. A form of mothering solidarity.

The bar gradually began to fill. A few people fresh off the lake, sunburns staking claim to their skin. Groups of barely-legal kids filtered in, and then the band, three men with Stratocasters and mullets, about their parents' age, started to warm up.

Joanna secured the dart board, said, "If we don't do something I'm going to fall asleep."

"Aw…I wish you could drink," Deb said, sucking on her last ice cubes. "I'm starting to feel pretty good."

Maggie's first dart barely hit the rim. "Still got it." She couldn't help looking around, though no one was watching, not even their old Civics teacher sitting next to the Mongoose and the Toad-Bear. Old Mr. Graybeck, who'd always had a line of yellow chalk on his crotch whenever he turned from the blackboard to address the class. She walked over and patted him on the shoulder.

"Hi there, Mr. Graybeck. Remember me?"

He, who appeared to still be wearing that same elbow-patched sports jacket, turned and looked at her. "If it isn't Maggie Johanssen, in the Buoy." He didn't seem all that surprised, even checked her out. "You've grown."

"Yes. It's all the cheese and beer in Milwaukee," she said.

"And the sausages," the Mongoose said. "You eat a lot of those?"

To her horror, Mr. Graybeck leaned back and laughed right in Maggie's face, beer foam half-covering his gray-mustached lip.

"Okay, well, real nice to see you," she said.

"Maggie." Mr. Graybeck wiped his mouth and peered at her more soberly. "I saw your picture in the Lumbertown Gazette. You're getting hitched soon, aren't you? Congratulations."

"Yeah," she said. "That's not happening. But thanks anyway, Mr. Graybeck."

* * *

"Your turn," Joanna said. "I'm whipping your drunk butts."

"If you two didn't still live here, I'd never come back," Maggie said. She'd reached her peak buzz-luck a few throws ago. Eight, she'd think, and the dart would hit eight. Bull's-eye, she thought, and the dart obeyed. But after her third beer, the darts arced out over the top of the board, clattered embarrassingly to the ground. "I'll get it back," she muttered. "I've just got to concentrate."

Deb ordered herself and Maggie another drink, and then the bar fell into darkness as the band played "More Than a Feeling." The stage show was lit by the same big can lights Maggie had directed onto their high school productions when she was part of the set-up crew. Blue, red, yellow, green. White smoke boiled out from a poor man's fog machine—hot water over dry ice in two five-gallon buckets—and was blown toward the crowd with a box fan.

They sat out the first song, but when the men struck up "Let's Go Crazy," and the lead singer sang, "Dearly beloved, we have gathered here today," Deb screeched, "On the floor, girls!" Maggie marveled at how each of them still had their own signature move. Even Joanna looked smooth, her style part marching band majorette, part snake charmer, exactly as it had been in high school. Deb had never been the most confident dancer, but the drinks seemed to inspire her, and she executed a few fancy foot slides and arm pumps.

Soon they were surrounded by people, smushed into a tighter circle.

Maggie was surprised to feel someone's hands on her waist, an assertive pelvis pressed against her backside, the breath in her ear all cigarettes and whiskey. She was ready to ninja the windpipe of whoever it was, all the Single Girls Self-Defense at the Milwaukee Y about to unleash. Instead she thought, this was how it felt to be a friendly young thing, open to experience, which is when she turned and pushed the Toad-Bear away.

"You can't just do that," she said.

He shrugged. "I kind of had to."

She gestured towards her friends, said, "We're just here to have fun."

"Right," he said. "Me too."

"Together," she said, throwing her arms out wide again, more wildly this time.

"Right," he said, and took a place in their circle and smiled like an idiot. Maggie shook her head and tried to ignore him.

It wasn't long before the Mongoose sauntered over too, his hands held up in front of him like a featherweight champ, leaning back and leading with his hips. He stunk of Brute, just like Eddie Ogilvy, whose locker had been next to Maggie's.

Deb must have forgotten that hard liquor had, in the past, led her to commit errors in judgment, because she held out her hand and the Mongoose took it and pulled her in close. Maggie wondered if Joe, driven mad by the scent of a rival male, would ravage Deb when she got home, disrobe her before she could even set down her keys on the entryway table. Maybe he'd throw her PTA blouse over the living room lamp, giving the room a bordello-like glow.

The Toad-Bear looked hopefully again at Maggie, who shook her head. "No thanks," she said, and wondered if she should save Deb from the embarrassment that would surely find her tomorrow.

"Leave her be," Joanna said into Maggie's ear. "It's harmless." Joanna reached out to the Toad-Bear and held him, middle school dance style, her hands on his shoulders, his hands on her hips, with plenty of room between for the swell of her growing belly.

"May I?" the Toad-Bear asked, and Joanna nodded. He held his hand flat on her stomach and kept it there until he felt the baby flip.

The band began to play an Otis Redding tune—"I don't want no cream and sugar, 'cause I've got you, now darling"—and the couples all leaned into one another. The air was thick with the smell of sweat and dry ice. The fog made everyone appear all Bogie and Bergman, lovers doomed soon to be separated.

If the two clowns hadn't run off to Baraboo together, Maggie would've worn a white dress this weekend. She and Roy had planned to get married in her parents' yard. Her mother had embraced the circus theme, rented a red-and-white striped big tent, bought miles of elephant-shaped plug-in lights, and sewed a lion costume for their cockapoo, Franky. Her dad had built a giant tower of logs near the pond, and he'd planned to light it just before his band, Steel Dreaming, covered the White Album in its entirety.

Maggie walked back into the other room. Behind the bar, Tammy was a blur of movement while two waitresses, who seemed to have appeared out of nowhere, waited anxiously for their drink orders.

"Tough night," Maggie said to a tiny blonde hoisting a tray of drinks, who couldn't get anyone to make way for her. "Let the lady through," Maggie yelled, and pushed at one mountain of a man until he focused his glazed eyes on Maggie's face. "What?" he asked her, but moved aside, and the girl entered the foggy room under her tippy load.

Maggie knew she was drunk, everyone around her, even Mr. Graybeck, getting younger and younger, almost as young as the kindergarteners in her class. Maybe she should pretend they were all five years old, that she was serving them chocolate milk and cookies, that soon they would nap. Or maybe she should duck behind the bar and help Tammy wash drink glasses. Build a pyramid of shiny tallboy glasses on a bar towel in front of Mr. Graybeck. Maybe she'd look different through all that refracting glass.

Doubting her ability to balance anything, Maggie instead found a seat in the shadows, her back against a wall, and watched her friends.

* * *

A few songs later, the Mongoose followed Deb and Maggie into the women's bathroom, pressed Deb against the air dryer, and said he was a Boy Scout looking to get his bathroom-fucking merit badge.

"Quit it," Deb said, in her best irritated mom voice, and slapped his stubbled cheek. "I'm a married woman."

"Don't worry, baby," the Mongoose said, stilling her slapping hand with his own and play-biting the air between them. "I'll get us some privacy. Nobody has to know."

"Yes, this is the perfect private spot," Maggie said. "Great idea, Mongoose."

"Who?" The Mongoose turned toward her with a sneer. "Oh, jealous, are we? Beat it, Chubby."

The Triumphant Return of Maggie Pancake

"You," Maggie said, low and serious, "you are the one who is leaving."

Because by then the Mongoose had returned his attentions to poor, trapped Deb, his spindly legs spread in what he must have felt was a position of strength, Maggie easily landed a from-behind knee blow to his gnads. When he crumpled to the bathroom floor, hurt as a child, Maggie briefly regretted her attack and moved to help him. But he rose from the floor on his own, feet slipping in his haste to leave, although he slowed long enough to curse their mothers and all the generations of women who'd come before.

And then Deb puked: all those lovely Long Island iced teas, all those mozzarella sticks. And while Deb emptied her belly behind a stall door, Maggie leaned into the mirror and tried to bring her reflection into focus. But instead of her own face, she saw Josie's: all the hair she'd lost in chemo returned, rich and brown, her bangs curled up tight like 1989.

"Looks like it's just you and me, kid," Maggie said as she rested her fevered head against that of her cool, mirrored friend.

* * *

The next day, after a late brunch, they brought berry wine coolers, Josie's favorite, to the cemetery. The syrupy malt alcohol burned their hungover stomachs, but each of them, even Joanna, drank one down. They poured the remaining three bottles on the ground for Josie. Afterward, they dropped Maggie off at her parents' house.

"I'm so sorry," Joanna said, gesturing to the monstrous bonfire tipi. "Roy's a bastard."

Deb nodded vigorously. "I knew he was wrong for you the minute I met him."

Maggie could see the concern on their faces and realized that concern had been there since Josie died. Josie had belonged to all of them, but she was Maggie's first and only best friend, even now. They knew and she knew there would be no replacement.

Maggie shrugged in agreement and gave her friends a squeeze. "Thanks for the night out," she said, and blew kisses as they drove away.

She needed a nap. Then she'd have enough energy to help her mother return the elephant lights. After dinner she'd douse the wood with gasoline, toss on a lit match, and let her parents tell her, over and over, how much they loved her. Somewhere in Wisconsin, the two clowns were happy or sad together, painting smiles and frowns on each other's faces. Maggie would have her own circus, masks and carnival music, great wild beasts to tame, and a cockapoo, looking for all the world like a lion in his golden velour mane.

Risen

When Vermilion Rex walked out of jail a semi-free man on a blue sky day in April, he told waiting reporters he'd found Jesus in his cell. "Despite my history of devious deeds," he said, "Jesus sat down on my bunk and forgave me. We both had a good cry." Indeed, Vermilion Rex had a history, one from which even the risen son of the almighty might have recoiled, but convincing jaded reporters was not his aim. Any criminal who has seen the light becomes a magnet for love and money, and Rex, as he always had done in his long public life, was positioning himself for a future of abundance.

After his pronouncement and before his baptismal public tour, Vermilion attended to his corporeal self, which had grown pale and dusty without its usual regimen of pampering. As he believed positively that success rained down from above, he first addressed his bleached helmet of 68-year-old hair. A white unknown to man, clipped to AstroTurf uniformity, gave him the look of a 1960s G.I. Joe doll: unreal, plastic, and indomitable. He kept his back to the salon mirror even after his preferred coif had been achieved, however, because the white would not slay until it found contrast in bronzed permatinted skin. The dye process used by the technicians at Gladiator Tan was not technically legal. The ladies who painted him with fuzzy rollers whispered about rare coral and jellyfish sting and pangolin gallbladder, but Vermilion knew enough about sales to suspect the ingredients were, in fact, toxic byproducts of some chemical industry. What did he care? We all die.

Next, of course, were the necessary push-ups, deadlifts, and anal Kegels—he liked occasionally to focus on more obscure muscles of his body, feeling this gave him hidden reserves of strength—but the dyes must set before he'd sweat overmuch or lap his own wake in the pool. And he stayed out of the sun, though he'd missed it while incarcerated. Golf-with-Money would have to wait until his plans were airtight and ready for the public.

Sexual release, however, he would not delay. First he accepted handjobs from the mini-dressed attendants (pre-roller) and then mouth service from his hairdresser, Lou, after which he hosted a small welcome home party with the usual deviants: 48 hours in his basement dungeon with all the nose candy one could ask for. Only then was he able to focus his attentions on selectively bruising his wife of thirty years, before a long-overdue midnight drive to the stables where he mounted his horse, Randy, through the bars of her stall. The shaft of moonlight that landed on her rump and made fairy sparkle out of the barn's suspended dust motes gave Vermilion his first involuntary moment of peace. The sigh that escaped him marked the transition between his recent past as a caged animal and his return to vitality and power: he was home.

Ground Truth

Len was a spotter, not a chaser. Although no one seemed to understand the difference. Storm chasers only looked out for themselves. They drummed up adrenaline, put themselves in the path of danger, cared nothing about the chaos they caused. All you had to do was watch the videos they posted of themselves, usually in idiot pairs. *Dude, it's a funnel cloud. It's dropping, it's dropping! Jesus fucking Christ, dude, it's touching down! Look at that debris cloud. Something just got BUSTED UP. Holy shit, dude, that's some huge hail. Ouch! Ouch! Get in the fucking car! Shit, we're too close! Go! Go!* They broke every letter of ACES, the spotter's code: Awareness, Communication, Escape Routes, Safety Zones.

As a member of the Washtenaw County Skywarn Spotter Detection Network, Len was always ready to be called into action. He didn't go looking for trouble. But he would report it as needed.

Which is why he had called Rose first thing, waited for her groggy morning voice, more familiar to him than his own, although it had been over a year since they'd woken up in the same bed. He gave her all the details: the storm prediction center in Grand Rapids had forecast an eighty-percent chance of severe storms developing near Ann Arbor that afternoon, gaining strength into the evening. High probability of large hail. High probability of tornadoes.

"It's six a.m., Len."

"Yes."

"If there are thunderstorms this evening, we've got quite a few hours to prepare."

"Yes, I thought so, too. That's why I called."

"No, I mean, Isabel has school. I have work." Rose waited. "The school sees the weather report. And they're not panicking."

"Who's panicking? The system's coming through between four and seven. Of course school's not canceled. But Izzy's party."

"Have you changed your mind? Are you coming?"

"Of course not," Len said. "I don't strap wheely things to my feet." Rose knew this. No wheels, no skates, no skis. Snowshoes, maybe, but only in an emergency.

Resistant. That was the word Rose used. Len was resistant to change. Once Izzy was big enough to more or less take care of herself—make her own breakfast, bike to a friend's house and back without supervision, send private messages mocking everything and everyone in the world—Rose had thought they should spice up their marriage. Skydiving, she said. But, Len said, ripcords amputate limbs. Lake Michigan diving, she said. Pinched air hoses, he said, the bends. The Appalachian Trail, she said, the Iditarod, Latin dance. Len said hillbilly murderers, climate change, and two left feet. Eventually Rose said leave.

The rift was her fault for prizing novelty over tranquility. Over certainty. Len was a known quantity, someone to be counted on. He refused to believe that was worth nothing in this world.

"Not even for your baby's big thirteen?" Rose asked.

"Put her on."

"She's still sleeping."

Len pictured Izzy in her pastel mushroom cloud of pillows and stuffed animals. *Isn't she too old to like this stuff?* he'd asked Rose last year when Izzy had begun to retrieve her old comfort items from storage, arranging them around herself before sleep. Rose said it was to be expected when a child's parents split up. Izzy needed protection from life's harsh realities.

"I should be there when she wakes up."

"I know, Len. I'm sorry. Maybe next year we can meet for breakfast."

"Have her call me before she gets on the bus." Len hated the way his voice sounded when he made these kinds of requests. Desperate and angry, hopeless, when he meant to play it cool, meant to show her how much he'd changed. "Rose, promise? Tell her about the storm."

She sighed. "I'll tell her you called, Len. I'll tell her you wished her a happy birthday."

Len felt his chances of convincing Rose slipping away. She was speaking to him in the warm but dismissive way she spoke to three-year-olds at Grundy's Tavern, the ones who asked for ice cream before they ate their dinners. *Oh, sweetheart. Oh, little lamb. You can't have that.*

"Reschedule the party."

"The deposit is non-refundable. Forget about the weather. Skate with your daughter."

"This is serious, Rose. This could be another Palm Sunday."

"Len."

"We're overdue for a really big one."

Silence. Then she threw him a bone. "They didn't have Doppler back then."

His old Rose was coming around, talking weather with him. He leapt on her generosity before she could withdraw it. "Or enough spotters!"

Ground Truth

"So you're on duty now, Len. We can all relax."

"Yes, I'll take care of it." He felt a small stomach jolt of pride. "Rose?"

"Yes, Len."

"Tell Izzy happy birthday."

* * *

On Palm Sunday, April 11, 1965, the first warm day of spring, the farm families of Indiana relaxed after church. They rolled up shirtsleeves, took picnic blankets outside, watched the children lay down palm fronds for Jesus' donkey, unaware that a cold front from the Rockies was about to collide spectacularly with air soaking wet from the Gulf. Inside the Severe Storms Forecasting Center in Kansas City, men in white shirts and dark ties prepared reports and studied charts. They suspected tornadoes would form, but cuts to the postwar spotter program meant there were few in the field to provide ground truth.

The first tornadoes downed the telephone lines, so there was no way to warn the towns to the east. Eighty-two tornadoes formed over the course of twelve hours. Two hundred and sixty people were killed, and more than three thousand injured. Schools became morgues, each citizen's car a hearse. When the full damage was known, people sent condolences from around the world.

* * *

Len called the department secretary, told her he had a virus and wouldn't be making any of the day's meetings. "Oh yes, you sound horrible," she said. "Is it by chance that wicked storm chaser virus that's going around?"

"I'm not a storm chaser," he said. "You know that."

"Of course not," she said. "You have the dreaded spotter fever."

Before his divorce, Len had not been subject to this level of derision. On potential tornado days, he'd pressed Rose to call in sick for him so he could scan the skies. Of course near the end she'd neglected this duty, along with all the others, said he was obsessed with disaster far out of proportion to its probability.

"Get better soon, Len," the secretary said.

* * *

Before packing his weather equipment in the car, Len jerked off to an old black-and-white picture of Rose, twenty-five and naked on a gingham picnic blanket. He'd been taking a photography class the year they'd met, and she seemed captivated by his large assortment of telephoto lenses, his 8x10 close-ups of falling-down barns and oak openings. *Do me next*, she said. So he did. Her dark hair in a thick braid against the pale of her shoulder. Her warm cello body. Her laughter at the intrusion of his large cylindrical eye.

It wasn't strange to imagine making love to this Rose, the one who wanted him. It felt like the most natural thing in the world. Black-and-white Rose was always satisfied, always grateful. She slept in his arms afterward, safe and sound.

* * *

Len wasn't a large man—what did he need with a large car? His four-door Accord, the safest in its class the fourth year running, suited him fine. Those storm chasers in their hulking tornado-proof SUVs were laughable, really. They seemed unable to understand that their elevation from the ground left them vulnerable to high winds, which would tip them with one stiff finger in any storm worth its special bulletin.

Denver, Rose's boyfriend, drove an SUV. A top-heavy Land Rover knockoff, built in Crimea, probably, by kidnapped reindeer herders. Len had warned Rose repeatedly not to let Isabel ride in that death trap, but she said they couldn't sell unsafe cars in the US; it was against the law. Sometimes Len thought Rose had forgotten everything he'd taught her during their fifteen-year marriage. What had she done with their old conversations, flushed them down the toilet? He'd even left her all their back issues of *Consumer Reports*, to protect her and Izzy, but now he wondered if she'd tossed them too.

In his passenger seat, a removable antenna. A signal flare. A plat map of Washtenaw County, section by section, laid out in reassuring squares, showing the Huron River, the five-block downtown laid out northwest to southeast along a river rise. On the town's northern edge, Skateworld, a long flat pole building with a metal roof curved like the top of a pig shelter. And on the river, Grundy's Tavern, a sprawler on stilts, its back deck a sunny paradise where you could watch fishermen and kayakers fight the slow current in their efforts to stay in one place.

In the back seat, a slicker and a pair of galoshes, bright yellow, size-twelve replicas of the ones he'd had as a child. *Classic*, he thought. Almost English. And also helpful should he ever be stranded on the side of the road. He'd be seen before impact. Or at least found quickly, in the worst circumstances.

* * *

"Len, you big fucking baby. You gotta lead her. She's the mother of your child, for chrissakes! I wouldn't let a woman do me like that." For emphasis, Fish sent his empty Bud Light in a high arc to the basket by his desk. A metal *plink* sounded as it landed on top of several others. "The world is big, my friend." He spread his hands wide across the expanse of sky they could see from his eagle's nest windows. "Why would you settle for one idiot woman when there's all this to choose from?"

Len could see no women—in fact, no people at all—from Fish's hilltop palace, a kit Quonset hut he had built in the eighties and from which he ran a personal ham radio empire. Len knew Fish had just recommended two contradictory maneuvers, but refrained from correcting him. When Fish got on a roll with advice, it was best to let him freestyle. Somewhere amidst all the bullshit, a few nuggets of truth would usually escape him, and you wanted to be there when it happened.

"Take me, for example," Fish said, leaning back in his faux-leather captain's chair, popping the footrest with gusto and adjusting a terrycloth towel behind his bad neck. "I put myself on top, see? With the best view. Nothing sneaks up on me. You, on the other hand, were so blinded by pussy you couldn't even tell when it was stepping out on you."

"I'm not blinded by pussy," Len said.

"Not anymore. Haven't seen none of it in how long? Exactly my point. So blinded by pussy you thought it was sitting next to you watching a movie, eating popcorn on the couch, when it was out with Colorado—that's his name, right? Nevada? Alaska?"

"Denver," Len said.

"DENVER! Denver's got your pussy. How can you stand that, man?"

Outside Fish's windows —not as transparent as a person would like, but panoramic, Len would give him that—the elongated repeating *S* of the Huron River entered and exited town, which from here appeared tiny and inconsequential. Their long view was interrupted when a male cardinal, slightly balding on top, landed on the window ledge. The bird stared in, its war-torn head bobbing left and right, then rose to attack the glass with its small and furious body.

At first, Len felt attacked, as if the bird was some sort of personal omen of things he'd done wrong, but then he realized the cardinal could not see him at all and was in fact fighting his own reflection. In the bright mirror of Fish's windows the bird saw a balding rival, his equal in vigor and paranoia. *"You'll never win,"* Len wanted to tell him. *"You've chosen a pointless quest."*

When Fish saw the bird he immediately took offense. As the poor creature bashed its wings and breast against the glass, Fish leaned his face in close.

"What the hell is wrong with you, motherfucker?" he said. "If these windows weren't special order I would hit you right between the eyes."

Len didn't think there was much real estate between the songbird's eyes, but he tried to keep a receptive look on his face.

Beyond the bird, who seemed determined to fight the window all day, clouds were gathering slow in the southwest. Though the wall of stubborn gray seemed almost stationary, an untamed wind was already cavorting at ground level. Wind that might stand up and break things before anyone had time to gauge it. Temperament like an independent woman.

Rose had been so young when they met. He had thought they'd grow and mature together into a hybrid of themselves, like an apple tree graft, maybe, where one variety of apple tree bore its fruit upon the roots of another. Any wild she had he could temper.

Why did these words share a derivation? *Temperamental, temper.* They seemed to mean each other's opposites. He would have tried to puzzle it out, but Fish kept talking and Len couldn't hold the thought.

When the conversation shifted to Fish's favorite conspiracy theory—he had maintained for years now that the government was quietly jailing all gun rights patriots in a maximum security prison in Iowa—Len excused himself to his spotter duties. Unbothered by the opening door, the male cardinal continued its assault on itself, but its mate sang out from a shrub by the Quonset hut steps. *Wiiit weeyoo weeyoo weeyoo.*

"You and me, little bird!" Len tried to sound gung-ho, confident, as though being out in a gathering storm was his idea of a really good time. But when he spoke the girl bird stopped singing immediately.

He had to put all his weight against Fish's door to get it closed. It wanted to rip loose and give itself to the wind and Len was just an impediment to its desire. Len was always trying to prevent something inevitable from happening. And failing. They could make inspirational posters of Len's failed tries. Shoulder against the rock of the world and all that.

The Accord let loose like a pinball down the washed-out gravel chute of Fish's 45-degree drive. He felt almost superhuman as he turned each high corner, like when he used to fly Izzy around—SuperBaby!—when she was six months old and chubby, and fit on the length of his forearm. She'd held her newly strong neck up over her dominion, her belly arched, her tiny toes pointed back, and she'd laughed as he swooped her through the air, through all the rooms of the house, lending her his mobility, his height, his strength.

"Slow down," Rose had said, the new mother and, at first, the more protective parent. "You're making me nervous."

But Len had scoffed. As if he would misjudge the velocity of the turn or the width of the doorway. Izzy knew. She trusted him absolutely. He was the safest ride in town.

His feeling of omnipotence faded as the slope gentled and was almost gone by the time his car slowed to a stop at the bottom of the hill, the tin octagon shaking its windy red head at him: *you fool, there's no one on this road for miles, and still, you follow the rules.*

* * *

As he drove toward town, Len considered the reasons Rose might be right about his hypervigilance. Dexter was not a tornado-free zip code, but at least it sat outside the giant C plotted out by Brooks, Doswell, and Kay in their groundbreaking 2003 study on tornado frequency. The C-shape, which stretched from Illinois to the high plains and south to Mississippi and the Florida panhandle, covered places which statistically had at least one tornado day per year, a day in which a tornado traveled within twenty-five miles.

And then there was tornado inflation to consider. With advances in technology and a boom in spotters, more tornadoes, even weak and temporary ones, were recorded. This made it seem as though tornado frequency was increasing exponentially when in fact the only thing that had increased was human perception.

Still, the numbers didn't lie. And they said tornado likely. Tornado today. Tornado, if anywhere, here.

As the gray wall stalked in from the west, ground-to-sky deep velvet doom, Len admired its imposing flanks, its textbook layers: the under light an ocean blue, the gray cat-paw line reaching out in the mid-ground, overtopped by a shout of bright glory. On the radio, Fish barked out the latest weather data, Wolfman Jack-style, along with call-in reports from other spotters and chasers. Usually, Len would have been spellbound by the chatter, but it all blended into one inconsequential hum as he drove toward his family.

* * *

Len didn't expect to be asked to pay when he entered Skateworld. Surely his Class 3 reflective rain jacket, dripping wet from the storm outside, signaled he was not there for recreation.

"I need to get inside," he said, aware that his voice had risen in pitch and irritation. "I need to find my wife, my daughter."

The man behind the ticket counter surveyed him, from jacket to golden galoshes, with bored eyes. "You can't wear your street shoes."

"This is an emergency. Don't you watch the weather?"

The man yawned.

"Then give me skates."

"Size?"

Len felt the anxiety that always hit him at bowling alleys, ski resorts, and skate rinks. He visualized the old, broken-down leather worn by everyone, the uniform men's and women's sizes, the stink and sweat accumulated from decades of people. All the things he tried so hard to avoid.

"Ten," he said, and almost fell over as he yanked off his rubber boots. He felt ridiculous standing there in his socks on the paisley carpet, which was dotted with permanent Bubblicious and orange pop and, he was sure, more than a little vomit. In the sky above him, though Len had taken his eyes off it, a storm advanced from the west at a lazy 10 mph. The tornadoes it formed were cloaked in rain. They spun because they wanted to, because they could. Because the conditions were favorable. They didn't care that Len's world was skating in circles under a flimsy tin roof, against his advice. They weren't concerned that Len had no control over his people, that his daughter was growing up, that his wife was not his wife.

In the middle of the rink—all old hardwood, like a high school basketball court, but curved and slightly tilted—Izzy and her friends had linked hands to form a chain. She was in the middle. One tiny but fast friend led the pack, stopped suddenly, and whipped the rest. Izzy's best friend, Mary, gigantic and in the most danger because of her greater mass and height, was loosed to the traffic of the outer circle. Len recognized the panic on the girl's face, the shock and inability to react. As she swung by, her wheels going out from under her, as she must have known they would, Len stepped out onto the boards. The other skaters parted before him as he rolled arrow-straight to Mary's side. She was crying and red-faced and had fallen hard on one elbow, and she looked at him as though he might be about to mock her inability to stay upright. As he raised her up, the rest of the girls surrounded him, whisked her away, and knit her back into the group. His daughter shot him a quick smile and a *Thanks, Dad* before they moved off like a school of wild minnows. From the sidelines, Rose waved to him. He dodged knee-high roller assassins as he skated to his wife.

Rose came in for a hug despite his wet jacket. "Look at you! You're in motion." Her laugh was genuine, he thought, not mocking. He decided he would take it.

In her presence, it was suddenly difficult to remember why he was here. "Where's Denver?"

Rose handed him Pokémon plates. "Help me set the table."

Len scanned the room as he laid out plates and napkins and ridiculously flimsy forks on the birthday tablecloth.

Children screamed with joy and danger and flashed by on their rolling wheels, but he didn't see Denver's golden head anywhere. That was a mercy.

"Rose," he said.

Before he could warn her, the music cut out (*It's ladies' night, oh, what a night*) and the rink DJ asked for silence so he could make a special announcement.

The glitter ball was still spinning, reflecting bright ovals of light across the now empty boards, when they heard the tornado approach. It was like a train, it's true what they say about that. Len realized it was too late to do what he came to do: rescue his child and his ex-wife, and drive them at a right angle to the storm, to safe distance, to a point of observation. He had imagined sharing some insider knowledge about the storm, which they would absorb with shocked and humble gratitude. They would see Len anew, realize they needed him in their lives—every day, all the time—realize that he wasn't to be discarded. They would find their way back to each other. Ditch Denver, buy new sheets, start again.

Where is the statue of Leonard "Len" Nelson? Would they tell the tale in later days, how he resisted his urge to push through the glass doors of the roller rink, run under a green sky to his Honda, and report on the most significant tornado Dexter, Michigan had ever seen? How he broke the spotter's code in almost every way? Stayed in danger when he had plenty of time to flee? Len knew Fish was up at his observation post, probably tracking him on the GPS and yelling into the radio for Len to get out of there, to *report, report, goddammit!*. Instead, Len knelt over his wife and daughter and her friends, his face close enough to Izzy's hair to smell her green apple shampoo, his bulk angled in an effort to receive the brunt of any incoming pain. They huddled together like huge puppies, heads hung low but eyes aimed toward the metal ceiling, expecting at any minute to see it peel off like a cartoon sardine can—*flooop!*

* * *

While the children and parents of Skateworld shouted in fear, and were spared, Len neglected to report the destruction of the northeastern neighborhood of Ivy Court. Hopping over the river—Len later pictured it joyfully hooting as it did so, some sort of meteorological cowboy god—the tornado found its groove on the flat, ordered streets of the suburb. It chewed up trees, splintered outbuildings, tore whole sides off two-story mini-mansions. Spears of wood and metal vaulted sideways to pierce the walls left standing. It concentrated on one, two, three houses in a row, then skipped over another, occasionally sidestepping to the left or right. In this way it created a fanciful pattern of its own design: a short-lived homewrecker, on stage for one night only and performing for maximum effect.

Afterwards, the neighborhood was open to the sky. The man who owned vending machines crowbarred the money out before any hooligans could rob him and shot venomous glares at every passerby. The big trees—the oaks and maples and basswood that had withstood a hundred years of storms—split in halves, top to bottom, or were pulled like garden weeds and laid down flat. Len walked around with nothing to do, nothing but to notice how many lives had changed, how many homes lay broken, the streets clogged with debris. How many angry, determined men were out with chainsaws, their heads bowed down to the tasks before them. Grief weaponized in their muscles, in the efforts they made towards order.

The destruction smelled like Christmas, when the workers at the lot made a fresh cut for you, cut off the hardened skin

so your tree could more easily soak up water in the stand.
All crushed-needle fragrance, the sawdust of recently living,
breathing beings. The trees that were half-down bothered
him the most: split in half but still connected to the ground,
still drawing water. One part whole though any observer
could see the project was doomed. Or should he feel worse
for those with *botas arribas*, boots and roots in the air? If
giants still walked the earth, perhaps these could easily be
repotted, helped to their feet by a large hand. That same
hand sprinkling tons of gravel and soil into the air pockets
then tamping down the earth, a parent tucking in a child:
there, there, the day is done, sweet dreams.

The Improviser

One minute he was singing grace notes, that proud-tail mockingbird in the sycamore, next he was pressed against the drive, held in a hawk's talons. And then he was nothing but four feathers on the ground. It was garbage day, and Janice in her house slippers, her hand on the bin's green handle, was the only witness. Which was fitting, as he was Janice's own mockingbird. He sang in her backyard tree, the only one that shaded her 8X24 fenced-in joke of a courtyard. She'd lived in Apt P for two months, so she didn't remember the swamp forest which used to fill the southwest acre. She didn't see the condo developers scrape the forest to field, pile the sticks and stumps in great mounds along the property line. She only knew what the neighbors had told her, that for days after the bulldozers opossum, raccoons, and snakes streamed through the complex, heading north toward the city park.

She was lucky to have the one tree, the mockingbird in its branches. His melodies belonged to other birds, but she wouldn't call him a mimic. An improviser, more like it, inspired by the lives around him. He seemed a blessing on her move. She'd left her husband of thirty-five years, left him everything: the house, the furniture, the Iowa snow and a shovel. *You're a bitch*, half of his messages said. *I love you, I miss you, come home*, said the other half. She played

The Improviser

each message until she understood the pattern, then erased them all.

Janice believed in life cycles, in the overall balance of predator to prey. So when the hawk took the mockingbird, her first thought was reverence, even gratitude. But then orange well-drilling trucks with orange ladders appeared on the southwest acre. They set their tungsten teeth to the ground, and their engines whined high and low like queasy chainsaws. Janice shut her windows, abandoned her backyard. She set up chairs in front, planted kale in clay pots, looked toward the north and listened.

A golden retriever charged in her front door, stole a ham sandwich and escaped. A widower brought her sweet wine, called her a stuck-up Yankee, asked her for some affection. Young men in the parking lot sat in cars and smoked dope. A couple strolled by in the evenings, swinging their toddler between them.

Squirrels colonized the sycamore. Hawks hunted in pairs, attacked bird feeders, chased songbirds into chimneys. Storm clouds built up from nothing, dropped six inches of rain on Louisiana. Her clay pots filled to their rims and overflowed. Ants invaded her bathroom. Janice sprayed them with vinegar and soap, left their bodies on the floor as a warning. More came. She bought poison. The ants brought it back to their queen. The wind picked up and Janice unpacked her sweaters. Her daughters called, and she told them about the weather. Told them to spend Christmas with their dad. Told them she'd be fine alone.

Hoist House

1.
Green Skins

Karl boasted he could snare two rabbits in one set. "Maybe three... no problem. Just watch me, Sadie," he said, and I rolled my eyes, thinking that anything more than a single rabbit was impossible during an average trapping day. At sixteen my brother Karl, short and strong, resembled our father. And, two years older than me, he'd roll up his shirtsleeves to give everyone in town a look at his biceps. Or he'd get rid of the shirt altogether, his muscles glistening in the sun, though mostly we were the only ones who got to see that.

Dead rabbits in all stages of undress populated the shed. The newest ones hung headless from the rafter beams, giving their blood to the dirt floor. The green skins, sleeve-pulled so the flesh showed on the outside and the fur hid within, soaked in pails of cold water. Later, Karl would rinse them under the well pump to flush out the last stains of blood. In other pails, rinsed pelts swam in solutions of salt and alum, weighed down with clean rocks so they couldn't float.

"That's right," Karl said, his thumbs massaging mink oil into a finished skin. "You looked at this batch? No holes. Perfect. I'll have my own *kaari* in no time."

A car, new clothes. There was no end to what he'd buy when he was rich. Each perfect pelt like money in the bank, though so far he'd spent most of it on hockey equipment—a new stick every year, an extra puck. If the Eveleth Reds called him up before graduation, he wouldn't look back. He'd put on his new jersey, sharpen his skates, and we'd travel up to the new Hippodrome in Eveleth to watch him play. He'd have a nickname by then. Finn Rocket, or Minnesota Miracle. Beautiful Bruiser, something like that; he'd leave it to his fans. I saw how Karl stroked the pelts, how they soothed him, not unlike the way the soft edges of our sister Lumi's blanket soothed her. I'd never say this to him, given that it wasn't forever ago that he last hit me with his fists, as he was prone to do when angry. Didn't matter who. Sister. Friend. All the same to him.

It was June, the ice long since melted, and our mother—we called her *Aiti*—slid her rabbit pie into the stovebox to cook and walked outside to meet us.

"You need *hairikutti*," she said, running her fingers over Karl's brushy head.

He ducked from under her hand. "*Ma.*"

"You listen to your mother, *sina tuhma poika!*" You bad boy.

Most fathers spoke English at work, but Aiti was one of the few Finnish mothers we knew who had set out to learn when her children started school.

He hoisted her over his shoulder and marched her around our yard of cut-off stumps, singing.

I propped her feet onto my shoulders, and we marched together as if my mother's body was a tree we'd just chopped down, the backs of her knees and thighs exposed.

She beat at Karl's back with the rolling pin, but she laughed too.

"Ai, she's killing me!" Karl said. "Let off from me, Aiti!" He made a big show of being beat down by our little mother, her eyes like a lynx. *Wild Kata*, as my father always said.

* * *

That afternoon it was too hot in the house and Karl was stained with the morning's work, so he and I brought Lumi, who was seven that summer, to the brook to swim.

A yellow-legged heron flew out before us, its slate-blue back dark as the shadowy woods.

"Lumi, did you see it?" we asked her, but she was interested only in things she could find herself. "I saw it yesterday, but I didn't want to tell you," she said. Then she returned to her own work, collecting shiny pebbles with her toes.

"Lumi," my brother said. "The crayfish are going to bite you." He moved toward her, his hands pinching like claws. "And here comes the biggest one, the granddaddy."

She screamed and grabbed hold of my waist, but Karl the crayfish was much too strong and he pulled her off to the deep pool, where he pretended to eat her.

"You should have saved me!" she yelled at me, her blonde hair tight to her head and dripping in her eyes. "You should always save your sister."

"But aren't you cooled off now?" I said. "Don't you feel better?"

She and Karl came at me then, both hunched over and pinching, and it was my turn to scream.

* * *

At four o'clock, when his shift at the Milford Mine was over, my father rode home in Einar Lohkenen's Model-T. They looked funny arriving at our gravel driveway, like two men who had tunneled out of prison and stolen a car. They were covered in iron dust, reddish black, the darkest splotch right under their noses where they'd breathed it up all day. And a line of clean skin where their hats had perched. Every day they rode the steel cage down 200 feet, below the sand and the rock with the other men: Czechs, Serbs, Irish, English, Italians and Finns like our father and Einar, all immigrants to Minnesota. Our father—our *Isa*—was always so much happier in the evening, another day below ground lived through, survived. Sweaty dirt-stiff pants and shirt left in the dry room at the mine for him to put on tomorrow, but home tonight was filled with dinner and sauna and Lumi laughing. Air that didn't stink of sulfur, or molder like a dead animal.

He told us sometimes about the miners' shack where he stayed before Aiti joined him in America. It was empty and small, and he could hear the wind through the wall cracks, pulling and pulling at the air in his stove until it woke him up.

"Why didn't you live in town?" we asked him.

"Later, I did. But that first winter, so tired and cold after the work? If I try to walk to town, I fall down in that road and freeze, and not one soul around to wake me."

* * *

At the foot of the oak tree, behind the chicken coop, at the edge of the cutover woods, Lumi found a rabbits' burrow that had been all dug up, the roof of leaves and sticks and soil pawed away. Five tiny heads nestled into five small bodies in a circle of brown fur. I figured we must have scared away whatever had been about to devour them. Or else it had left with a larger meal.

"Their mother, she'll come back," Lumi said.

I shook my head.

"Mother rabbits are good fighters," she insisted. "They'd never leave their babies. Not even if a fox came."

"Or a coyote?" I said. "Or a wolf?"

She picked up one of the babies. The others squeaked in protest and moved closer together to fill the gap. The rabbit shivered in Lumi's palm.

"I'll be their mother," she said, and placed them one by one in the skirt of her dress.

"Ooh la!" Isa said, when we walked into the house. "Lumi the ballerina is showing us her underpants."

Aiti clucked and moved to fix her skirt but Lumi stopped her. "Look."

"Oh, Lumi. What you find now?"

Karl peeked inside. "A beautiful bunny scarf for you," he said, and Lumi pulled the corners of her skirt even tighter, exposing more of herself. "They're going to live," she said.

Isa brought the *kantele* out of its case, laid it on his legs, and began to sing. His left hand lay light on the strings, the tips of his fingernails black against the golden wood. In his right hand, a thin stick, which he swished back and forth like a broom.

Lumi believed the stories we told her. All of them. Even the one about the gigantic woman who rolled her body inside the first ocean to create the world. And the one about the man who jumped into the water to lay with that giantess. Lumi sang along in her high voice and, after settling the rabbits down in a box by the fire, she stomped her feet and danced to the rhythm of the words.

* * *

On the Fourth of July, two weeks after Karl had tanned the baby rabbits' hides, three weeks after the morning Lumi woke the house shouting when she found all five dead in the box, Einar Lohkenen arrived at our house with a crate full of chickens. "You pick your best," he told Lumi. "There are very many beautiful ones. Green eggs, brown, spots. What color you like?"

She said "All the colors!" and Einar laughed.

"Of course. Mama, you want all the colors for this little one?"

"We need just two, Lumi," our mother said. "Or you will gather eggs from our shoes."

Einar had on his dirt mustache from the mine, but it was hard to see under the gray and black hedge he grew above his lip. Lumi looked for it nonetheless, held his face tight in her small hands, peered as close as she could. Einar's forehead held permanent creases which he could make wriggle, like earthworms. Lumi touched them lightly with her finger and squealed when they moved.

Our father said Einar was too smart to keep his mouth shut. And that when the Iron Range miners formed a big strike in 1916, Einar joined the other men who took up their picks and shovels, turned off their carbide lamps, and walked out. Nothing came of it, though, Isa said. They still worked ten-hour days, and Saturdays.

After Einar left, Lumi built a chicken house with wood scraps and old lath, and filled the cracks with mud.

"Where's the chickens' door?" Karl asked.

She scooped up her two chicks and dropped them in through the open roof. "There."

"We need to get to town," I said. I had been washed and dressed for hours, and Karl and I seemed to be the only ones who cared that it was a holiday. Hiski Salomaa was coming over from Michigan's copper country to play that night at the Workers' Hall. Word spread secretly from person to person, because the mine owners considered him a rabble-rouser. He'd been jailed as a conscientious objector during the war, and his songs, if you understood Finnish, were meant to incite the workers to fight together. That's what Isa said, anyway. All I cared about was that there'd be music all night. In my mind, my plain white dress became a red silken one, and I pictured the great singer pointing to me and asking me to join him on stage. "My little Finn fire engine," he might say. "We've been waiting for you. Please, sing for us."

"Town? Tsss," my mother said. "Town ladies, they do nothing but talk. Flattened fingers," she said, and held up her own round ones to show me. "You know why? They bring washing on that porch to see those neighbors and they talk so much—ha!—their hands go in that wringer." She nodded for emphasis. "Just look next time. Some of those ladies, they paint their fingernails to hide 'em. Or give up, and hire a good Finn girl to do that wash."

I said nothing, and she smiled.

"Oh! So my Sadie, she wanna paint her nails, bob her hair. Wear store dresses cost a whole month's pay. You got rich pockets I think."

I blushed, wondering if she could see the dreams inside my head: my red dress, the stage.

"Sadie and Karl, you Finn-Yanks, you get out of here," my father yelled from the step. "Go to town. Your Aiti and Lumi and I, we'll be here, having fun without you."

"No, no!" Lumi cried. "I want to go, too."

Even hermits like Einar went to town to celebrate the Fourth of July, and so, like everyone else, we got ready and walked those two miles into town, falling in with our neighbors along the way.

Crosby's Main Street had been cleared of cars, and people had taken their place. Miners, farmers and loggers mixed with town folk and fancy people, everybody smiling and acting friendly.

Isa split from us when he saw men he knew outside the Workers' Hall. Before the women were sent for, the men spent their extra hours building this place. Father lived in the boarding house then, and that's where he met Einar. All bachelors—*poikka mies*—as father said. I watched my father and his friends, so animated, though someone must have told a joke at my father's expense, given how the rest leaned back, laughing and miming the raising of a drink, and one or two patted my father's back. But then he smiled and joined in the laughter.

Karl was antsy. He wore his best white shirt—he'd even asked Aiti to iron it for him—and a new cap he thought made him look sharp. He had a large pimple on his chin that he'd sworn at earlier in the hand mirror. I saw him dab it with a little wet clay before we left the house, but the covering had already worn off and the pimple shone red and angry, like a tiny volcano about to erupt. As soon as he saw his friends, he left us too.

"Lucky we get some rain to settle this dust," my mother said, as cars and horses passed by on Main Street. I liked seeing her in her best summer dress, her hair shining and pinned up in the back. Her dry hands she could do nothing about, and they took turns covering each other. The wives and children also gathered around the Hall, the women's voices speaking the mother tongue, quick and musical, like birds, and their faces relaxed, freed from the careful work of English.

Soon the grand firemen's parade started, led by the Merry Maids club, each young woman dressed in a crepe paper costume: one a daisy, one a violet, another a rose. Then the soldiers walked by in formation. Old men from the Civil War, just a few of them left, helped along by a much larger group of recent veterans. A draft horse pulled a cannon behind as it had, the day before, a plow. Riding the horse was a young blind soldier with only one leg, eyes staring straight ahead. Lumi pointed at him and said loudly, "What's wrong with that man?"

I placed my hands over her hands and pressed them on her heart. I worried for children who saw too many frightening things. It changed them. I saw it happen. When Emma Matechek's mother died, we watched the horses pull the carriage down the street, her open coffin on it. We stared at her, Karl and I, and her face was so pale. She just lay there, this woman we had never seen still in our lives. Emma buried her head in her father's shoulder, her legs wrapped around his waist. When she finally met his eyes he used his palm to wipe her face and set her down by his side, where she stayed, right tight to him. But I could tell—anybody could—the part of her that believed in every happiness her mother had ever prepared for her, that part did not exist anymore.

* * *

"Give me a swig of that," Karl said, and hidden flasks flashed silver from so many pockets.

In the Workers' Hall, my brother stood with the rest of the Barn Owls hockey team. Graceful and powerful on the ice, so large in their layers of padding, they seemed without skills on the dance floor. Corn liquor had to do, and the boys who had it passed it to others, their night's fortunes sewn together by a shared thread of moonshine.

Our parents stepped by in a fast waltz, Isa's hand spread wide on the small of Aiti's back, and her hair falling loose around her face and her mouth open in a laugh.

I stood with the older girls, who talked and laughed loudly, bending over with each next joke. They could barely stand still in their dress shoes with all that air swirling around their bare legs. Blood rose in their cheeks, the boys with their flasks and those hungry eyes on them.

"I'll do it, dammit," Karl said, and raised a fist to the boys who'd pushed him out toward the ship of open floor to the girls' side, his sleeves rolled up and shirt unbuttoned so his tanned chest showed through.

"Ladies," he said. "How are we tonight?"

The girls met him with a cloud of giggles.

I don't know why he always tried for the tall ones, but he did, holding out his hand to one of the Magnuson girls, an easy six inches taller than Karl in her bare feet. A dangerous tower in her mother's black heels. In an act meant to amaze his friends, he stood close, stared right down into her cleavage, and gave her a big smirk. "May I?" he said, and whether it was the peek at her bosom, his lack of height, or his pimple, I don't know, but when Metta Magnuson blushed and refused my brother, his smile turned to a sneer in approximately one second. "*Perkele,*" he swore, and tossed a mean look at me too, just for being there.

"Her loss," his friends told him. "This dance stinks. Let's get out of here."

I stayed and kept to the shadows, and Hiski Salomaa sang "Värssyjä Sieltä Ja Täältä," "Verses From Here And There": *There are five hundred thousand Finns living here, in Uncle Sam's country as of this year.*

As Hiski sang, another boy asked Metta Magnuson to dance, and this time she said yes. He was tall and thin, and held her as though she were as breakable as an egg. The men gathered around Hiski as he sang, pumping their fists in agreement with his words, his parted black hair about to lift off from his head like two ravens. But I watched Metta and the boy, and wondered if someone would look at me that way, and when. I watched them until my parents stopped dancing, scooped up Lumi from the pile of coats she'd been sleeping on, and told me it was time to go.

"What about Karl?" Lumi said sleepily from Isa's shoulder.

"Your brother's off with his friends," Isa said. "He'll find his own way home."

* * *

The rest of that July, low clouds and humidity kept the mosquitoes close and loud. One morning Aiti and Lumi brought food to a neighbor who'd just had a baby girl, and left me to chores. I scrubbed the kitchen floor and an hour later it was still wet. I hung the wash on the line and deer flies bit me everywhere my skin was exposed, leaving welts that itched and ached. As I weeded the garden, a hummingbird dipped its beak into a radish flower, its deep green body dropping to a bent fish tail.

Karl sat on the back step and watched me work, barely concentrating on the pelt in his lap. To break a skin you needed to work one small area at a time, pulling it in all directions until it turned white and limp.

"Don't you have anything to do?" I said.

"Why, you going to tell?"

I pictured the cool insides of the big houses in town. If I lived in one I'd wake up in an upstairs bedroom all my own, with a door to shut out the world. I'd lie in that bed undisturbed until I felt hungry, then go downstairs still in my dressing gown and laugh with my sisters (I'd have only sisters) over coffee and omelets and toast with peach jam.

"Hoo! Look what I can see!" Karl pointed at the too-tight front of my old dress. "You're in the mood for a boyfriend now, huh?"

"You're disgusting," I said, and stood up from the rows and walked to the pump to wash the dirt from my hands.

He might have left me alone then, but as I went back into the house I couldn't help myself. "At least someday I'll *have* a boyfriend. But what girl will ever want someone as pimple-faced and stupid as you?"

He caught me upstairs just as I reached the bedroom we children shared, and wedged my arm behind my back and held it there, his voice hot in my ear. "You think you're so smart, Sadie. But who's smartest now?" He pushed me close to the window and said, "Maybe I should throw you out."

"*Stop*, Karl," I said, and twisted in his grasp, but he forced my arm up higher until I cried out, and when we fell onto the bed, he pinned me with his body, which smelled of fur and skins.

"Get off!"

He brushed the hair from my face and tucked it behind my ear. "You're almost a real girl now, Sadie. Let's see if there's anything here for your future boyfriend to care about. I'll do you a favor and check." He leaned back just a little and his free hand moved from my waist up to my ribs and higher.

His face changed then. It relaxed, and for a second his eyes closed as his hand continued to move.

We didn't hear her come up the stairs, but suddenly my mother's voice rang out behind us. "You *will* not. You *will* not," she said, her voice growing louder with each repetition.

She said it as she lunged at my brother and dragged him by the hair off of me onto the floor. She said it as she bent over him, and again as she hit his back and head with her fists. Her voice seemed heavy in her throat, as if she were pushing a stuck horse from the mud.

Then she turned to me, and her eyes were wild and unseeing. "You! Get out. Get *out* of here!"

I ran down the stairs and into the garden. The zucchini blossoms opened their orange mouths, and the bridal flower of the green beans, courted by a swarm of fat bees, was no cover for me at all.

* * *

The trail to the heron rookery was only a deer path, collections of shiny pellets all along it, crushed grass to the sides, under pines, where they slept. The bugs chased me, and spider webs clung to my hair and forehead. By the time I emerged from the forest to the beaver pond, the whole world knew I was coming.

Herons stood up on their great nests of sticks atop each dead tree, stretched their long legs beneath them to appear taller. Their wings, spread wide, cast shadows on the few overgrown babies, their squawking fuzz turned to feathers, and already too big for their nests.

I brought my hand to my chest and left it there, trying to feel what Karl had. Why it mattered. But it was impossible to separate what my brother felt from my body's sensation of being touched. I tried to silence my skin, tried to touch myself like I touched the stump I sat on.

I traced the path Karl had taken on my body, wondering if a boy I liked would someday touch me with the same anger Karl had. Cause me pain, force me? I thought of the boy at the dance, the shy, tender way he stood back from his partner, barely able to meet her eyes. The way he took her hand in his, and, with the other, touched her back. The exact opposite of what my brother had done. What if boys were only gentle when people could see them? And in the dark rooms they did what they pleased, whether a girl wanted them to or not.

A beaver moved in the water in front of me, its wet head making a steady V in the still pond. Its tiny eyes cut toward me, then it raised its paddle tail, slapped a warning, and dove.

* * *

My mother was on her hands and knees scrubbing the kitchen floor when I returned.

"I washed it already," I said.

"Well, you must not have done a very good job." She pushed the rag against the floorboards as if they had done her some wrong, her back and arms tight.

"Where's Karl?" I asked. I pictured him at the top of the stairs, waiting for me.

"In the coop," she said. "For all tonight."

I looked out the window and saw she had barred the door from the outside. I'd walked right by it on my way back to the house, but he'd made no sound.

"What's he's doing in there?" I asked.

"Maybe he makes feather bonnets for us, to show he is sorry."

"And is he...sorry?"

"He says so." She kept scrubbing. "If not, he will." She grabbed my ankle before I could walk away. "You don't want it. What he did. You don't invite him." Her hand was wet and hard on my skin.

I didn't know what she meant. *Invite.* I shook my head *no* and wished I could let out the scream I felt inside me. *Invite.*

"Who did you invite?" Lumi at the door, her dress covered in dust. "The chickens are being so noisy. And I can't get in to check them."

"Karl is in the coop," my mother told her.

"I'll let him out."

"No. He plays a game. See if those kukko can be calm with a person in there. How many eggs they lay. He comes out early, we never know. And you stay out too, Lumi, till this floor is dry. Run off, find something to do."

"But I already *did*."

Aiti shook the rag at her. If she was forced to get off the floor to make you mind, you were in trouble. Lumi flew out into the yard just in time.

* * *

When Isa got home, Aiti said calm as you please that Karl had gone camping with a friend.

"Where to?" Isa said.

"Oh, I should know, Aarne?" she said, heaping another slice of rabbit pie onto his already full plate. "Who knows where that boy goes."

"To the pond," I said. "I think."

"Mosquitos will eat him alive," Isa said. "Lumi, your brother will look like he's got chicken pox."

Lumi's eyes lit up. "Yes, he *will* have chicken pox, because..." but I kicked her knee under the table at the same instant that Aiti pulled back Lumi's chair and said, "Time for bath, you muddy girl. Off we go."

That night I lay in the bed with Lumi sprawled at my side, sheets kicked off. A fat moon shone in our window, and it made hard shadows of our dresser and door. It shone on Karl's first place ribbon, the one he got this winter when his team, the Crosby Barn Owls, beat the Aitkin Icemen. My own show poster of a Japanese Geisha, the one my Uncle Matti brought back from a merchant ship, was half lit, so I couldn't see her white painted face or her red lips. The flowers on her kimono, perfect white lotuses, were their own glowing moons in a sea of black silk. Here and there, on the edges of our things, Lumi had tucked in dandelions and violets. She forgot to take them down when they wilted, so dead flowers hung their heads over the geisha's shining black hair, and cast shadows on Karl's furs and ribbons.

A pack of coyotes began their conference in the woods, yipping higher and higher as they moved closer to our house. I lay wide awake listening to them, and imagined Karl did too.

Which brother should I condemn? The one who created a rabbit fur dress and miniature snowshoes for my doll the Christmas he was ten and I was eight? That wooden girl came alive when I dressed her in the things he'd made.

Or the brother who locked me in the root cellar, among the jars of jam and piles of potatoes, the musty smell of earth wrapped around me, my heartbeat in my ears? The feeling that I'd used up all the air and would never breathe or feel the sun on my face again? And then his face peering in the open door, the gap between his front teeth and his big smile. "Oh, did I forget you here?"

* * *

The cat groomed herself in the sun by the coop. Lumi and I watched as she curved her spine to attend to the fur on her back leg.

"She licks where she poops," Lumi said.

"She has nothing else to wipe with."

Lumi scrunched up her nose. "*Yäk.*"

Lumi and I had been sitting outside the coop since sun-up. We thought our mother would come let Karl out then, right away, but she stayed inside for a long time. Finally, she walked towards us, wiping her hands on her apron. We helped her pull the bar, and she opened the door.

Out flew a few outraged chickens, fussing and clucking. Out came Lumi's half-grown chicks, molty and awkward as they grew their new feathers. Lumi chased after them with her arms outstretched. "Come, chicks! I'll give you a bath. Come, chickie-chickoo!"

It was difficult to say what kind of creature my brother had become, curled on the chickens' top bench, asleep with his back to the birds. His hands covered his ears, hay woven through his hair, and white and gray chicken poop all over his clothes. I saw scratches on his bare arms. I thought, from his face, he might have been crying.

He sneezed: once, twice, and a third one that jerked his whole body.

When our father first built the coop, Karl and I used to play in there. We got in trouble then, too, for getting so dirty, for disturbing the birds.

"Karl! How many eggs did they lay?" Lumi asked. When he didn't answer, she pushed by us and tugged on his leg. "Come on! The experiment is over. Come out and I'll count the eggs for you."

When he did get up, he refused to look at us. We stepped back and let him pass into the sunlight, trailing dust and hay, smelling sharp like bird droppings. He kept his elbows tucked tight to his body so he wouldn't touch any of us.

* * *

Lumi filled her bucket at the pump, her body almost lifted off the ground by the handle's rising. She brought the water to a hollow in the dirt and poured. She made ponds and floods. She liquified the earth.

"Here is the pond. Here is the mine. Here go the men." She dropped in pine cones and sticks. "Here is the iron." She dredged up gravel from the bottom and poured it onto dry land. "Here are the fathers. Come up, fathers!" Up through the mud they rose, covered in it.

"How do they breathe?" she asked herself. "I don't know."

2.
Pie

Karl packed a knapsack with venison jerky and wire snares and disappeared into the woods. As I did my chores under a dull, punishing sun, I half-expected him to saunter back out from the thick stand of young poplars that encircled our house and our cut-stumped yard, but he stayed gone. From the woodpile, Karl's hatchet seemed to accuse me—*Why have you made such a fuss?*—its honed blade half-buried in the oak log, its handle worn shiny by the sweat of his palms. By late afternoon, my father on his way home, nobody needed to tell me to hide. I took the steps two at a time to my room and watched the driveway from the window.

Einar stopped the car and Isa stepped out into a cloud of dust, my mother right there waiting. I couldn't see her face, but I could tell by the way Einar stepped on the gas and drove off that bad things might be coming. As Aiti spoke, Isa stood motionless, but then when he tried to push her aside, she leaned in and held both his shoulders. He seemed okay, even nodded once, but then he turned suddenly and flung his lunch pail in a high arc, raised his palms to her, and stalked off back down the road toward town.

He didn't return for dinner, and neither did Karl. That night, the moon lit up the buildings that capped the Milford Mine—the headframe, the hoist house—tall gray and smoke blue in its slow rise skyward. And my father and brother bright as ghosts as they walked into our yard at midnight.

Isa stomped up the stairs to our bedroom saying, "Kata! Sadie! Wake up now!"

I heard my mother rise from bed, say, "Aarne Marttila, what you are doing? Is the middle of night!"

Middle of the night or not, we gathered downstairs, my father already in his chair. He said, "Here is the plan," and he waggled his finger in front of our faces. "It is time for you to help out your mother and me, much more now. Karl, you go to the mine with me tomorrow. And you, Sadie, no more a young girl. We find work for you somewhere."

With this, my father's eyes began to close, though we all just stood there, as if the moonlight through the window had cast us like that, a bronze replica of a family forever shamed, our mother barefoot in her nightdress, her hair escaping from her braids. Finally she said, "And that is all you say, Aarne?"

My father waved a hand lazily in the air, as if conducting a lullaby, and so we left him there to sleep.

* * *

After supper the next day, my father said, "Oh, don't you look at me that way, Sadie. It is for the best, you'll see. Best for you, too." He corralled my neck in the crook of his arm and pulled me close. He smelled of liquor, not a lot, and also of wood and sweat.

And to Karl, "Come, boy!" he said. "The men sauna first."

I washed up the dishes with my mother.

After a while, she spoke. "Maybe he is right."

My throat tightened, and I squeezed my eyes shut and said, "You want me gone?"

She placed her hand on mine in the dishwater, her fingers blurry salamanders. "You know this answer," she said, and removed her hand and dried another dish. "I make for my daughters many wishes. If you learn a new thing, you are luckier even than me." She laughed then, and gestured around her with both hands. "All this, I've got!" she said. "All this we build. Yes?"

I nodded.

"But. But...a girl makes money. She says what will happen. To her family. Yes? And maybe you give part just to me? I keep it safe. Our secret." She looked me in the eyes. "Sadie. Your brother, he is young. He spends his pay. A big man, your brother." She puffed out her chest and tucked her thumbs in her apron strings. "A big rooster!" she said, and I laughed as she strutted around the room, her knees pushing out sideways from beneath her skirt.

* * *

Karl hunched over the breakfast table, the gray wool Harvard golf cap he'd ordered out of the Sears catalog for 47 cents shading his eyes. He'd cleared all his things from our bedroom, and it made me sad to see them piled in a heap on his low bed in the corner of the kitchen.

"Today, you do only timbers," my father said. "You work with Einar, okay?"

Karl scowled at his eggs and nodded.

"You don't be a tough guy. You stay with Einar."

"I know, Isa."

Aiti clanked the tops on twin lunch pails and pressed her hands flat on the tops.

"You check him, Aarne."

"You think I won't, Kata?" Isa sighed. "Eat those *munat*, Karl. Or your mother, she gonna come down into the mineshaft herself."

Karl smiled just a little.

"You come right home," she said. "No drinking."

"Ah, Kata. It's his first day."

"He drinks it here." She turned to face them. "Dandelion wine. Even whiskey. At home."

"Your mother, Karl. She scares even me."

Einar's horn brought both men to their feet, but before Karl took a single step, my mother buried her face in his neck, then handed him his lunchpail and pushed him away. "You are careful."

"Good luck," I said, and Karl nodded, looking directly at me for the first time since it happened. Lumi, who'd been awakened by the horn and stumbled downstairs to say goodbye to Isa, as she always did, cried out when she saw that Karl was leaving too. She didn't want to let go of his leg, but Aiti untangled her and wiped her eyes.

"I'll be fine," he said. "I'm your tough big brother," and he rolled up his sleeve to show Lumi his chopping muscles.

"Tough all right. Tough in the head," my father said, and cuffed Karl's hat over his eyes.

We followed them out the door and watched the first orange light of morning filter through the trees. Our men would be underground before the sun cleared the tops.

My brother's back was a smaller version of my father's, but not by much. They walked identically, slowly, as if wanting never to arrive at Einar's car.

* * *

We heard them laughing as they drove up to the house. They wore the clothes they'd left in, but they looked like different men after a full day of labor, their shoulders moving easily in their joints, their faces relaxed now in the sun and wind. My brother swung his empty lunchpail in one hand, light as air.

The mine had a bathing house where all the men showered and changed after their shifts, but even so, I saw that his face was already slightly stained with earth, and smudged by the miner's lamp still on his forehead.

When Karl picked up Lumi and twirled her around, she kissed first one cheek and then the other.

"You were worried about me?" He pinched her nose and set her down. "There's nothing to worry about, little sister."

"Oh, hell," Einar said. "Your brother, he did the work of ten men today. It's like he was born underground. Like an earthworm."

Einar, Karl, and my father collapsed into the wooden chairs in the yard. They took off their boots and socks and propped up their feet on three stumps. "Lumi, come rub our feet!" Isa said, but she screamed and ran away from their wet wiggling toes.

Isa laughed. "But he did have *paskahousu* on his first trip down in the cage." Dirty pants. Something you said when a baby needed his diaper changed.

Karl's face turned dark red.

"Really?" Lumi asked.

Einar joined in tormenting my brother. "The guys made noises like we were falling, saying, *We're all going to die!* Karl, he let out a few squeaks, I tell you."

Karl stuffed a huge pinch of snuff under his lower lip. "I wasn't scared."

Einar and Isa howled and made high-pitched frightened noises at each other until the cat ran out from under Einar's chair.

"Kata!" my father called. "We are so thirsty! We may die soon!"

She brought all three men, each of them, a large jar of honey wine, which Karl drained in one uninterrupted gulp, as if proving how long he could hold his breath, then wiped his mouth with the back of his hand.

* * *

I did small things first. Pulled a button off Karl's best shirt. Took Aiti's shears and cut a hole in his new cap. Emptied his snuff onto the ground for the chickens to eat. At first that was enough, and I felt a rush of excitement punishing him. But Aiti sewed on another button, the hole in his hat too small to matter. He bought a new tin of Copenhagen with his first paycheck, walked around like a big man, even cockier than before.

That's when I got my most terrible idea. I made small apple pies, and fluted their crusts into pretty ridges and dips. And into part of the filling I mixed dandelion tea at triple strength, a half-cup of castor oil, and extra brown sugar and cinnamon. On top, the letter K, cut out of dough. On the other four pies, the ones I hadn't tampered with, I put an L for Lumi, I for Isa, A for Aiti, and an S for me.

We ate the crusted pies, still hot and steaming, that same night.

"What'd you put in here, Sadie?" Karl said. "Too much of everything. Did you pour every jar in there?"

"Don't eat it," I said.

"Oh, I'll eat it," he said, and he made a big show of licking his plate when he was through. But then he grimaced, and quickly poured himself another glass of milk.

I was distracted the next day thinking of Karl down in the drifts, working side by side with Isa. As contract miners, they were paid for the iron they loaded each day, not for their time, and Isa said the crosscut they were in was bad ore, hard as steel. The dynamite that should have busted the rock into small pieces they could shovel out instead left puckered holes in the wall. The miners called them "assholes," a term Isa shared at the supper table so Aiti would swat him with her kitchen towel. "The children, Aarne!"

They were hoping to move to the new section of the mine soon, even though it was wetter. "At least then we get paid for some *helvetten* ore," Isa said.

I pictured Karl down there in the darkness for ten hours straight. I wanted to feel bad for him, but thought, *He can suffer a little. He can be a smaller person for once.*

* * *

"Shit himself."

"*Aarne.*"

"No other way to say it, Kata. Our boy shit himself so many times he should have left his pants off." He shook his head. "I never seen so much *paska* come out one man's body. I tell you, we did not want to let him in the car. I make him sit on his jacket. We drove home with the windows down and still it stinks like holy hell in there."

I listened from the upstairs window.

"Poor boy. Where he is now?"

"Where do you think?" Isa gestured towards the outhouse. "You'll need to go somewhere else today."

Aiti walked slowly to the outhouse, raised her hand to knock, but must have thought better of it. Instead, she stood there for a few minutes, then walked back into the house after my father.

I don't know if Karl stayed in the outhouse all night or not. By the time I woke the next morning, he was standing alone at the edge of the yard, burning his ruined clothes. I dressed and went out to stand near him. "Are you okay, Karl?"

"Jesus, Sadie," he said, poking at the fire and shaking his head. "I must have really pissed God off." He gave me what could have been a smile. "Go on in. You don't want to get too close to me right now."

3.
Mummo and the Buffalo

There it was, dark and shiny. And our father behind the wheel of a brand-new 1923 Ford Model-T.

I could feel my mother's anger, the silent intensity of her displeasure obvious to everyone but my father, armored by the signing of the loan papers at the bank, by his visions of ever-increasing prosperity. He was, for the moment, impervious to disenchantment or harm.

"I didn't rob your egg money, woman. Go check. It's still there."

She stamped her foot on the driveway, but we children were bound by no such money worries, and escaped our mother's wrath by battling to be first into the car. Lumi squished in next to Isa, and Karl and I elbowed our way into the back.

"Let's go fast and never stop!" Lumi said. "Even on the bumpiest roads, I'll hold it for this ride."

Isa squeezed the rubber horn—*ah ooh gah*—and we began to move, his feet dancing a polka on the three pedals, and I worried for a moment that we might hit our furious mother.

"You stop it, Aarne," she said, turning in place as we circled, and with each slow pass he grinned at her, his eyes wide as silver dollars. Then he raised his eyebrows and winked like a lonely young man looking for a date.

"Come on, pretty lady, take a ride with me. Through the mountains and valleys, the plains and seas."

She wiped at her eyes and called him a *ryokale*, a scoundrel. "Well, you wait for me, then. I have to change."

* * *

We didn't see mountains or seas that day, but a few weeks later Isa drove us to the edge of the plains, on the south road along the edge of the Mississippi, to visit our Stearns County relatives. "You are the navigator, Aiti," Isa said, handing her the brand new map of the Trunk Highways of Minnesota, each main road a thick red line. The Portland cement highways were mostly flat, except for those bumps of poured slab the tires slopped over every ten seconds or so. Isa put on the speed for us, our hair whipping round our eyes and into our mouths, but he slowed down after he discovered, the hard way, that the road wasn't wide enough for two cars at a time.

"You bring us here to kill us, Aarne?" Aiti asked, after we'd been run off the road by a milk truck. "This exactly what happens to a reckless man, buys a car without telling his wife."

Isa craned his neck to see under the car, his good shoes deep in the cattail muck of the ditch. "Not stuck too bad," he said.

Karl stood beside him. "You've got a scratch."

"What? Where?" Isa asked, bumping his head on the side mirror in his haste to rise. He rubbed his thumb along the offending mark, which only grew more pronounced with his ministrations. "Goddammit," he said. "Karl, give me that gunk of yours."

Karl's hair pomade smelled like a beaver's ripe musk glands, but it was dark and oily thick.

"Ah," Isa said, as he dabbed it gently over the scratch. "See that? Good as new."

Aiti scooched into the driver's seat, ready to steer, and called Lumi in from the ditch, where she'd been making mud pies. "Sadie, wash your sister's hands," she said. "And you boys, push!"

* * *

We stopped for a picnic where the Crow Wing River met the Mississippi. *Gaagaagiwigwani-ziibi*, Raven Feather River, Einar's girlfriend Judy had called it. Off and on for the past four years, he'd been courting a girl from Mille Lacs, who he visited every Sunday. Isa said, "The slowest growing up man I ever met. Be seventy before he kisses her. Maybe put a hand up her skirt on his deathbed." We knew that where these rivers came together, there used to be a town, almost a hundred years vanished by the time we got there.

"But there's nothing here," Lumi said, expecting to see Ojibwe women rising from the water to tip Dakota warriors' canoes. Karl thought there'd be piles of fur tall as a man, loggers walking the surface of the river on rafts of pine. And I imagined Chief Hole-In-The-Day with his beautiful face and fine clothes, just back from a tour in Washington, or maybe see Indians packing up their things to leave for the White Earth Reservation, way up on the North Dakota border. Events I'd read about in school.

But it was flat land, a picnic table underneath a willow, kids fishing the channel by the big island at the junction of the rivers, the one that was supposed to look like a raven's wing. We had cold bread and butter. Gingersnaps, ham.

"Strange, isn't it?" Isa said. "How they lay the train tracks elsewhere and this place not so important anymore. They took apart the buildings, and they move them too."

"They wouldn't move our town," Lumi said. "Right?"

"Might. Found ore under Main Street in Hibbing, so they put the houses on skids and moved the whole thing. Iron right there below the surface, easy as opening this picnic basket. But me? I am one of the last digging moles, a *kemmooli*," and he leaned over Lumi, his eyes closed and his hands splayed out by his face.

I imagined him tunneling into the mounds by the river, where the Indians had been buried, the sloped sides so smooth that Lumi had an easy roll to the bottom, which she did over and over again.

Another two road hours landed us at Uncle Matti and Aunt Hazel's, Tallboy Nelson's farm, really, but our uncle ran it for him, and he and our aunt and our little cousin Lars lived in the white farmhouse with the wrap-around porch in the middle of acres and acres of tasseled out, whispering corn. Isa and Matti's mother, who we called Mummo, had arrived last year to join them.

Isa's younger brother got the height in the family, and a hearty manner that made it seem like he'd been born here. In those days, according to my father, the Russians were drafting all the young men, and no self-respecting Finn wanted to die for a czar. Matti had jumped ship in New York after his first voyage as a conscripted sailor and, as far as we knew, he was still a wanted man. He'd made his way to our place when Karl and I were little, tried mining for a bit, but couldn't abide that kind of work, dark and wet, and, like he said, with no sense of his own worth. He married Hazel instead, a dark-haired German girl whose parents lived on a nearby farm. It didn't take long for him to get to know his neighbors and, eventually, Tallboy Nelson. Pretty soon he was doing well for himself.

Hoist House

The addition of Mummo to the household could've gone badly, my parents thought, except that Hazel didn't speak enough Finnish to understand what Mummo said about her cooking, or the way she was raising her child.

Isa sped up and honked his horn as we drove up to the house, the dust flying in great swarms behind us. Out onto the porch to greet us came Matti and Hazel, Lars and Mummo. The brothers spent some time kicking the car's tires, but soon enough we all sat together in the kitchen with pie and coffee. Lumi drank some of Aiti's when she wasn't looking, and her eyes cut this way and that like a hawk's as she flew around the house with Lars. Mummo packed tobacco into her corncob pipe and lit it with a blue-tipped match. She took a couple hard puffs in quick succession and blew perfect rings above the heads of her grandchildren, who leapt up and grabbed them from the air.

Mummo always dressed in black. The only one in our family who went to church, she treated Christianity like a present and a weapon that had been given only to her. Her husband had been a sinner, she said, and he gave her two boys who were also sinners, and she would have to pray for the rest of her life to save them. And if sometimes she lapsed and fell into their wickedness, God would surely understand. Jesus enjoyed the company of sinners while he was on the earth, and she guessed she did, too.

"You want to try the new batch?" Matti said, and pulled aside a checked curtain from a cupboard to reveal shelf after shelf filled with pottery jugs, the farm being a real farm but also a distillery. The best illegal whiskey in the country, Minnesota 13, came from this county and its short-season corn, and my uncle was just the man to help brew it.

"Ei sylkeä lasiin," Isa said. I wouldn't spit in the glass.

The adults each took a small portion. I stood behind my mother, and watched her tilt her head back quick and yelp.

"Worth the ride down," Isa said, after he finished his.

"You are my husband's sons," Mummo said, motioning to Matti to refill her glass. "Blood half liquor."

When the children were sent outside to sleep in a big canvas tent, Karl stayed up playing cards with the men on the porch, still taking sips from the bottle and getting louder.

"Wanna play for money?" he said, and we heard the clink of coins on the table.

"Watch out," Matti said. "Word is I can't be beat."

"You never played with me."

Isa cleared his throat.

"Let the boy try," Matti laughed, "he's such a hotshot."

We got cozy in the tent, pulling a light quilt over us, and listening to the men.

"What if we were out on the plains," Lumi said, "and a herd of buffalo was headed our way right now."

"They'd go around us," I said.

"Or trample us!" Lars said. Lumi, like a huge moth in her white nightdress, hopped on top of her cousin and pummeled him.

"Your elbows, they're so bony! Get off!"

* * *

"My luck again, Karl," Matti said. "Slide me those pennies, if you would."

"Should of brought my own cards," Karl said, low and surly.

"You think I marked the deck is why you're losing?" Matti laughed.

"Watch your mouth, Karl," Isa said. "Your uncle doesn't cheat."

"Have another drink, maybe your luck will change," Matti said. He still laughed, but there was a warning there, and I wondered if Karl was too drunk to hear it.

"Once there was a pocket of land with no people," I said, trying to keep the children from hearing too much of the men's game. "It was circled by high mountains, so high no one could climb them, and inside was a field of sweet grass, and a clear cold lake, a rocky stream that tumbled down the mountainside. Hot summers, frozen winters, and the only animal suited to living there was the buffalo."

"See! There again. No way in hell you keep getting cards like that."

"Maybe you should crawl into your crib and let the big boys play," Matti said, and this time Isa stayed silent.

"And the buffalo that lived there, they'd lived there forever," I said. "Shaggier in the winter, lazier in the heat, more stubborn in the cold, and they called themselves the kings of all creatures. They bellowed at the birds that flew high overhead, thinking they could take them down with their voices."

Lumi and Lars lay still in the dark of the tent, their eyes half-lidded.

"Goddamn bullshit fucking motherstoker!" Karl howled, and the men roared with laughter as Karl stumbled off the porch in a shower of profanity. "*Perseennuolija*! *Helvetti*! *PERKELE*!"

"Karl!" my mother called from an upstairs window. "You shut up down there. You hear me?"

A rooster woke and tried a crow, as if morning had arrived ahead of schedule.

"Ah, shut up, you noisy devil, you," Matti said to the rooster. And to Karl, "Maybe cards aren't your game."

"*Voi perse*! You don't play fair!" Karl said. "*Vittu*!"

The screened door banged open and Mummo's walking stick rapped hard on the porch. "It's after midnight, you *piru*, and this is the day of the Lord. Get to sleep or I'll hide you all."

Lumi and Lars had moon eyes again, and we listened to Karl being sick, and the men chuckling, "It's all right, Mummo," Matti said. "We're done for the night."

"What happened next, Sadie?" Lumi said.

"People climbed the mountains. At first a lot of buffalo died, because they didn't know about hunters, but eventually they learned to keep their heads down and run fast. And after a while, they learned to trample."

* * *

The next morning, we stepped over Karl on our way into the house: drool from his open mouth and his arms around the farm dog curled next to him, the sunrise lighting him pink. Lumi and Lars giggled, and Karl snorted, but didn't wake.

"We'll try to come down again for Thanksgiving," Aiti said.

"Thanksgiving?" Mummo said. "You should give the thanks every day. You give God the glory."

"We know, Mummo, but this is an American holiday."

"Holy day! What you know about any holy day? I am the only one walking to church." She batted softly at her sons with her cane, hitting one's shoulders, the back of the other's knees. "All these children growing with no fear of God. You should be ashamed."

"Come, child," Mummo gestured to Lumi, who came over cautiously, most likely wondering if she, too, would get swatted. "Come look at this creche. You know who these are?"

"It's the Baby Jesus."

"Good, good. That's right. And this?"

"The Virgin Mary."

"Yes! God put a baby in her belly before she got married. A miracle."

Lumi placed her hand on her own belly, worried again.

"Oh, God's already done that once, child. He's not going to give you that kind of gift." Mummo laughed. "And you're lucky. What a surprise. Can you imagine Mary telling her family? That girl, she got hit a lot before they believed her.

"Do you think you might want to be a nun, either of you girls?" Her blue eyes all squinty, we couldn't tell if she wanted us to say yes or no. We shook our heads. "That's all right. There's no shame in a life of marriage. Even Jesus needed a mother."

"And a father," Matti said.

"Well..." Mummo let the word fade, as if unwilling to weigh in on the usefulness of men. "A heavenly one, at least."

She whisked crumbs from her mouth with a napkin, then rose, stood on her pointed, polished boots, plucked a man's felt hat from a hook on the wall, and said, "If Jesus comes while I'm at church, I guess it's too bad for you."

"We'll do God's work here, Mummo," Matti said, but she just extended her small swollen-knuckled hand.

"The offering, son."

Matti pulled a crisp dollar from his pocket and Mummo tucked it into the top of her dress.

I thought then of Jesus tiptoeing over to the farm when he didn't find us at church, everyone's names and addresses in his head, which maybe explained why he looked like he had a headache in so many of those paintings.

Karl, who staggered in from the porch after Mummo tapped him on the hind end with her stick, would not impress Jesus today.

"How much did you lose?" I asked him, but he only grunted and chewed a piece of bread.

"You let him play for money, Aarne?" Aiti said, her voice filled with Old Testament judgment.

"It's good for him to know, Kata, that you don't always win."

After breakfast, Uncle Matti brought Isa and Karl out to see the distillery, and I let the children talk me into a game of hide-and-seek. Lars knew all the best places, but they decided to hide together, and neither could last thirty seconds before shouting out, "Pssst. Hey, you! Long-legs. Nobody here. Come see!"

"Enough of this," I said, and found them giggling in a mostly empty watering trough. "You need to learn to play this right. You stay here and I'll hide. Count to fifty. No peeking."

I ran to the side entrance of the house, into the dirt room where they hung up their working clothes, and hid behind the coats, my feet tucked into a pair of slop boots. I buried my hand in the pocket of my uncle's coat to keep it from giving me away and thought at first a mouse had made its home there. At the bottom of the pocket were layers and layers of paper. But when no small teeth bit my fingers, I carefully peeled off one of the papers and let in a little light to be sure I'd seen right. A blue seal. A picture of John J. Knox. *National Currency. 100 Dollars.*

My breath got hot and loud behind the thick coat, and I started to sweat. I knew I should stop but I dipped my hand in again and brought out the whole mouse nest of money. All new bills. 100. 100. 100... I thumbed the stack to hear the soft thump of so much cash. Maybe because I couldn't believe it was real, I put it all back except for one. It almost didn't feel like stealing, there was so much, more than a lifetime of Aiti's egg money, or even my father's paychecks.

I folded the bill I'd taken into the tiniest square and tucked it into my shoe. I could hear the children calling for me outside. "Sadie! You cheater. Where are you?"

I'd start my new job at the grocery right after we got home. Maybe Aiti would take all of what I made, but even if she didn't, I could work a million Saturdays and never save a hundred dollars.

Folded up small, it felt like nothing. Nothing to miss, nothing to feel bad about. It wasn't as if I was going to spend it. A girl like me, going into a store with a hundred dollar bill? A kind of loan, that's what it was, a good luck, just-in-case, emergency treasure. Maybe some time in the future, I could save the day, and everyone, even my aunt and uncle would say, "Sadie, our girl! How ever did you become so smart and brave?"

* * *

When we left Uncle Matti's farm late that morning, our new car was packed tight with crates of whiskey. At first Aiti refused to get in, but she couldn't make a fuss in front of Isa's family. She sighed like a long-suffering saint when she realized that she'd have to sit cross-legged the whole way home.

"Just enough to pay for the car," Isa told her, when we were a few miles down the road.

"And what you give him for it?"

"I'm good for it."

"You didn't pay him?"

He waved off her question and became suddenly interested in the countryside. "Look out there, Lumi! Cows!"

Lumi said she wanted the creamy white and brown one. "We'd call it Leipajuusto," she said, which meant "bread cheese" or "squeaky cheese," for the sound it made when you chewed it.

"You don't understand commerce, Kata," Isa said. "You get a hundred—no, a thousand—times profit for this whiskey. And for us, it's almost free." He hit his palm against the wheel. "If you ever want a cow, goddammit, Kata, you got to untie a man's hands." My mother had wanted a cow for years, but somehow the money she saved to buy one always disappeared.

Lumi fell asleep on my shoulder, her hair smelling of sweet exertion and warm fields. Karl groaned every time we hit a bump, or turned a corner, his rank breath filling the backseat. Sun flooded in through the rectangular back window, but the burn I felt came from the money in my shoe, and I tapped my foot against a whiskey crate to settle the itch. I smiled to myself until Karl punched me in the shoulder, and even that couldn't change my mood.

A cow, I thought. *Maybe sooner than you think.*

4.
Chorus of Inspired Damsels

Isa and Karl unloaded the whiskey in the back shed and covered it in bales of hay. Isa had wanted it stored in the house, where he would feel safer about it, but Aiti found him moving her good dishes to make room for the liquor and raised such a stink Isa didn't even bother talking back. He just put each dish back as if he'd only been taking them out to look at his reflection in their shiny porcelain surfaces. They put an extra wooden bar on the shed door and Isa bought a combination lock.

    At the Workers' Hall, Isa had quieter conversations with different men, men who wrote penciled directions on scraps of paper and handed them to him. Handshakes and eye-to-eye nods. Karl stood back and looked unfriendly. The men might have been worried by his demeanor if he hadn't obviously been just a boy, and one they knew.

    Aiti stayed far on the other side, her back to her men. After a while, she pulled my father away, talking quiet, her head tilted to tell him something privately. He pulled his arm free and turned back to the men. She stood there, back straight, watching him, probably counting the seconds in her head until he turned back around. But he didn't. He threw his arms out, gesturing to make a point. He rolled his shoulders back, as if shrugging off an unpleasant worry.

He laughed, and Aiti turned quick when she heard it. In a minute we were gathered and out the door.

"The car," Lumi said, tired on her late night feet. "I want to ride with Isa."

"Oh no, the car is for big men," Aiti said, giving one of its wheels a little kick as we passed it. I almost ran into her when she turned on her heels. She reached into the cab and squeezed the rubber horn.

"*Aiti*." She was doing this just to embarrass me, I was sure. "Lumi, come on. You can ride on my back."

"Naw," she said, her face lit up. Aiti was finally acting like a kid. Why leave now?

A couple of people came out of the hall, but not Isa. Aiti climbed into the driver's seat and hit the horn again.

Isa came out, Karl at his shoulder, both their arms crossed. Isa swore a little when he saw Aiti in the car, then tromped over, opened the door, and scooted her over with the bulk of his body. Aiti stared straight ahead with a little smile and said nothing. All the shadows looked long and menacing on the silent moonlight ride home. Isa stopped the car at the turn to our driveway and left it running. "Out," he said. "Not you, Karl. We've got work to do."

* * *

On the first Saturday in August, Aiti plaited my hair so tight, and secured it with so many pins, I felt like Mummo's Jesus with his crown of thorns. After submerging my hands in the breakfast dishwater and attacking them with her bristle scrubber, Aiti smoothed my fingernails with scouring reeds she'd harvested from the stream bank. Lumi seemed pleased that for once I was the subject of Aiti's ministrations, and she cackled at my scowls and wounded cries.

Aiti even bought me real stockings with her egg money, though she'd spent the last year telling me I was too young to wear them. She showed me how to hike them up my legs and fasten the clips in back, and swatted Lumi when she came up behind us and said, "Ooh! La di da di da. A real lady from Paris, Sadie."

"Yes," Aiti said, once she'd finished with me. "Your sister *is* a lady, isn't she."

Then Aiti and I hiked the two miles to town, the morning birds loudly commenting on my appearance and the orange sun peeking over the trees to see what all the fuss was about.

My bread and butter breakfast sat heavy in my stomach, and I practically had to run to keep pace with Aiti's rhythmic step. "Hurry up, slow poke," she said, and went on and on about the letter she'd written to her parents back in Finland, telling me how proud they'd be to hear their American granddaughter was a working girl now.

Before I knew it, we stood in front of Kaminski's Grocery on Main Street. Dozens of yellow jackets lay drowsy on the harlequin apples arranged in baskets outside the door, the ripe fruit intoxicating them so they couldn't even fly away.

The store windows were framed in red, white and blue bunting, and filled with sea-green bottles of Coca-Cola, tins of National Biscuits, and high piles of oranges, lemons, and bright purple cabbage. A stenciled sign said WE PAY CASH FOR POULTRY, EGGS, AND BUTTER.

I felt it might be wise to stand outside for a while, peep through the windows and get my bearings, but Aiti opened the door right away and set the bell jangling, announcing our presence. With every step I wanted to sink into the floorboards, which were thin and pitched slightly to one side, and darkened by the dirty shoes of the town.

Aiti pinched my upper arm and pushed me ahead of her towards the proprietress.

Mrs. Kaminski leaned back so she could look down her nose at me through her reading glasses.

"You're the Marttila girl."

I nodded and pointed to my mother, who'd left me standing alone while she stared at a corner display of Rinso detergent.

"And you're mute," her laugh a blast of dynamite.

Maybe she felt sorry for the way she had scared me, because she took me in her arms and pressed me to her pickle barrel body.

"Kata!" she yelled out. "Your girl, she doesn't have your spunk."

My mother walked over to us. "Don't be fooled, Elena. All of us, we have the spunk, all right. And Sadie, she is very hard worker. I make sure of this."

"Then you belong on this side, little duckling," Mrs. Kaminski said, and when I came around she collared me with a white apron.

Aiti set her purse on the counter, said, "Now ask me what would I like."

She bought a pound of coffee for 47 cents, a single cabbage for two cents, and one tin of Norwegian Sardines in Olive Oil for 15 cents. I located each item, some high up, some low in the four rows of shelves that lined the store's walls. Mrs. Kaminski tore off a length of paper from the large roll perched on an iron spindle. "Like so," she said, as she wrapped and tied, then Aiti asked her, "And what, Elena, for us something new and exciting, something rich to try?"

"Reese's," she said. "They put the peanut butter right inside. So delicious," and as they gabbed on about the candy, the hairpins dug deeper into my scalp, the fabric of my new stockings slouching down into my shoes as if I'd already been working for a full day.

"We'll try not to tire out your girl too much."

"Oh, you will please not worry," Aiti said. "It is why she is here," and she carefully counted the coins and placed them in my cupped palm. "Thank you, Miss," she said, and, without another word, she was out the door.

Sam, the Kaminskis' tall and dark-haired oldest son, chuckled, his height half-hidden behind the printed sheets that served as curtains, separating the store from the stairway to the family's upstairs apartment.

"Oh, shush," Mrs. Kaminski said, "and listen up. Nettie Johnson says give her a watermelon, a half-gallon of milk, macaroni, butter, and a pound of caramel wafers. And she says bring the new Wonder Bread, and to let yourself in with the key in the flowerpot. The hooligans, she thinks, are coming to steal her furniture."

All day I packed the groceries for each order, and after Sam finally left with the last one, Mrs. Kaminski locked the door and went upstairs to count the till. She left me to clean up, and I listened to the sound of a piano and two girls singing upstairs as I wiped the front of the glass cases and swept sand and gravel from the floor. I'd just begun to dust cans of fruit when I heard giggles behind me on the stairs.

"Hello, Sadie. Are you doing my parents' bidding?" Merva Kaminski said as she took an apple from the bin, her sister Celia a Baby Ruth. "Don't worry, they won't blame you. And don't stop because of us."

I turned red and wished again to disappear. These girls were no longer just my schoolmates, but also my bosses' daughters, and I decided the best thing to do was to stand still and say nothing. Merva, who at school was known as

Marvelous, hopped up onto the counter and took a loud bite from the apple, leaving a red mark where her lipstick had rubbed off. I pictured myself with that color—a bright swatch, my mouth a cardinal—but it didn't fit. You'd have to change everything else about me too. Curl my hair and make it thicker, wave it with elaborate fingers and setting cream. *Her* hair smelled of lily-of-the-valley, her dress, a pressed sailor white. Celia was quieter, everything about her more muted. But Marvelous Kaminski seemed the sort who might, at a moment's notice, pack a trunk and board a ship, even star in a silent film, opposite a kohl-eyed man under the stars and moon, dancing cheek-to-cheek on a deck marked by pockets of light and shadow.

"What did you think of our singing?" Celia asked, but I stayed silent.

"The Chorus of Inspired Damsels?" Marvelous said.

I shook my head.

"Oh, now we've scared her," Marvelous said. "Let's see. Maybe she could audition with London Bridge? Except we don't know for sure if she *speaks* English."

"I speak English," I said, my voice weak and halting. They looked at each other skeptically.

"Ellen!" Marvelous shouted up the stairway.

"What?"

"The hired girl is sick. Come down here."

The youngest sister, who appeared to be about nine, poked her head through the curtains and looked at me. "What's wrong with her?"

"Just watch the store. Five minutes. Ten, tops."

It was wrong to let a child do my job for me, especially on my first day of work, but I followed Celia and Marvelous up the stairs. Celia wore tweed knickers, a long sweater, and her brown bob bounced as she climbed. When she smiled back at me over her shoulder, she radiated her own kind of beauty, even if it wasn't as loud as her sister's.

The stairs were narrow, dark, and steep, but at the top, a window seat with a cushion and a wall of books. In a south-facing room flooded with light, a grandfather clock, the floor rug-covered.

Mr. Kaminski sat in a great stuffed armchair reading the paper, his feet propped on a padded footstool with golden beads and feet like wooden lions. I imagined my own father sitting there, slippers on his feet. Smiling.

"Come now, stand here," Marvelous said. "There's a good girl. You know Euripides? *The Bacchae*? It's about bad girls who dance naked in a forest."

Mr. Kaminski cleared his throat, said, "Describe it properly, at least."

"Dad, it's an *ancient* play. It's about the god Dionysus, and the women who follow and worship him. It's the school play. And we need more singers. Better?"

"Just barely," Mr. Kaminski said.

Celia sat down at the piano. Marvelous stood next to me, her arm linked in mine as if we'd been friends forever. "I'll start, so you can hear how it goes."

Celia played and Marvelous sang in a rich soprano, Celia in high harmony on the chorus.

"And now you."

I pressed my lips together, still held the duster in my hands like Lady Liberty's torch. Maybe this was a test, and Mr. Kaminski was deciding whether or not to fire me. Celia played the opening notes. I thought of Isa at home playing the kantele, how easy it was to hear the music and to join in. But here, with strangers? I closed my eyes, and I sang.

* * *

"Come down!" Ellen said, and we did, the three of us still singing, "The Wild Maids of the Hill!"

Aiti and Lumi stood just inside the door and suddenly I could see their shabbiness. My mother's coat, seasons old, had a bit of sawdust on one elbow where she couldn't see it, and her shoes were dusty from the long walk. I wanted to see her the way she'd seen herself when she'd left the house. Visiting clothes. The best clothes. Clean and pressed, for a special occasion, picking me up after my first day.

"Please, you tell your mother thank you very much. My Sadie, she is appreciating the work."

She walked so fast on the way back I had to hurry to keep up, and we were out of town before she spoke.

"I brought you something," she said, handing me a still-warm raisin bun wrapped in cloth. "But maybe you don't need it, since you play upstairs today."

"They asked me to come up," I said.

"They ask you not to work?" she said, and walked faster, Lumi skipping ahead.

"There's a play," I said.

"There's a play, there's a play," she mocked, and forced a small, angry laugh. "I don't know this talk, this play."

"I do!" Lumi said, and I added, "They said maybe I could be in it."

* * *

Aiti set her mouth all through dinner, wouldn't let me help with dishes afterwards, spoke to the air instead. "Sadie the singer, too tired to help here at home."

"You fill it up like this," Isa said, and tapped chunks of dusty carbide into the reservoir of his Auto-Lite lamp. "Gotta keep it dry, son."

Karl made a noise like he was going to spit, but swallowed it when Aiti glared at him. "You forget that I know more than a little about the carbide."

"Jesus, boy," Isa said, and laughed. "You make a bomb out of it, nobody gonna work with you."

When they were kids, Karl and his pal Phil Angello terrorized the troops of Kaiser Wilhelm in the forest near our house, setting up pine cone soldiers and bombing them with homemade explosives, tin cans filled with stolen carbide, thick string fuses.

No one minded too much, until Karl got the bright idea to set off a charge behind crazy Miss Papineau's outhouse while she was having her morning session. And after which she came marching over, shouting French curses. Aiti had to settle her down with coffee cake, and Karl was whipped so hard he never touched the carbide again, at least not anywhere our parents could see.

"You know, Sadie, she get her voice from me," Aiti said, facing her reflection in the dark window, holding a wet plate in her hands.

"Ah, now...that's true," Isa said, and set down the lamp and its fuel, and patted his knee. "Come here and sing for me, my Kata."

She held the dish up, and Isa said, "Let Sadie finish them."

I took the dish from my mother, and Lumi took her hand and led her the rest of the way. Karl concentrated on his own golden lamp, frowning as he dropped in a couple gray pieces of carbide, fitted the felt filter to its rubber gasket, and pretended to ignore the conversation. Aiti looked like a shy girl on my father's lap, burying her face into the hollow where his neck met his shoulders, as he retold the story of how they met.

"I heard your mother before I saw her. Like a siren, a *merenneito*, she seduced me with song. I was a defenseless boy," Isa said, "and she seduced me."

"Not so. You are the one with the bad ideas. But the song, what was I singing?"

"*The Golden Fleece.*"

She hit at his head. "No!"

"Eh! Woman! Of course you were singing *The Last Boat to Shore.* You think I'd forget that?"

"You never would," she agreed, and they brought their faces close.

Lumi couldn't take it anymore, said, "Let's get to the singing!"

"And she wore an ironed white shirt buttoned all the way to the top and a blue apron over it, embroidered with red flowers."

Karl snorted.

"Shows what you know," Isa said. "But you will. And watch that…you're spilling."

"What about shoes?" Lumi asked. "What shoes did Aiti have on?"

"Oh, I guess I don't remember that. But her legs, the little I could see above her shoes, and below her skirt, that seemed a gift from heaven."

"Her legs?" Lumi sounded disappointed, so Isa told her the rest, how he leaned over the fence and stared at her as she walked by. How he did it again when she walked back that afternoon and how she aimed a smile at her shoes. And how, a few days later, he mustered the nerve to sidle up alongside her, ask if he could carry her basket, keep her company on the walk to town. Aiti mumbled, "*If-you-want-to,*" and Isa said back, "*You-bet-I-want-to,*" and it wasn't too long before she let him tickle that bit of skin above her shoes with a wheat stem he'd pulled from her father's field.

"You tickled her?" Lumi crowed.

"Wasn't that brave of me?"

Karl snorted again.

"You're going to blow us to Kingdom Come, son. Half-full is plenty. Now fill the extra can, too. Pretty much all I thought about down in the mine was tickling her, and saving enough to bring her here."

"Don't you dare," Aiti said, as he lifted her skirt hem just a little, his fingertips dancing up her calf. It didn't take Lumi long to launch herself at Aiti's other leg, while she kicked at them and threatened consequences.

"Say you'll sing," Isa said, "and we'll let you up, woman."

"She'll sing! She'll sing! All of us will sing!" Lumi shouted, and Karl said, "Kaboom," to the lamp on his lap.

"So. You watch. This is how I do," Aiti said, and stood statue straight, her hands tight on her ribs, as if preventing her insides from escaping. She tilted her chin up and sang in Finnish:

> *Go to sleep, bird of grass*
> *Get tired, wagtail*
> *Sleep while I'm putting you to sleep*
> *Get tired when I'm making you tired.*

Her voice caught on the last line and her back grew stiff.

The day Aatami died, Aiti closed her bedroom door and kept the rest of us out. Karl and I lay on the floor just outside her room and listened to her sing lullabies for hours. Later, when Isa found us asleep, he placed his index finger to his lips and led us downstairs.

Aiti shook herself, as if she'd caught a shiver, and turned to me, a dull, stubborn cast to her eyes. "If you sing bad, you know, you can quit." I must have looked hurt because she said, "What? You sing here, in a forest, with birds listening. You sing, sing, sing. Look at this," and she poked at a picture in the *Crosby Miners' News*.

A bunch of Crosby's puffed-up bigshots: the caption identified them as Dancing Thunder Tribe No. 163, I. O. R. M. (International Order of Red Men). They stood shoulder to shoulder in the new opera house, shiny sashes across their chests, hair slicked back from their pale foreheads, in front of a large audience. Grecian columns lined the walls, and frescoes of dancing girls filled the ceiling.

"You'll be afraid in front of so many," Aiti said. "Mark my words."

"Ah, Kata," Isa sighed. "It's late, too late for this worry. And our girl has her first job." He tugged on Aiti's skirt until she softened her gaze. "Karl, bring that here." Isa set his lips around the burner tip and blew. "Good. No leaks. Screw it together now. Ya, ya. Not so tight. You'll strip the threads."

Aiti excavated the Reese's Peanut Butter Cups from her purse, broke up the chocolate pies, and gave us each a piece. As the candy melted on my tongue, and despite my mother's warning, I felt that somewhere nearby a future me was opening her mouth, and rows and rows of people were filing into a great hall to listen.

5.
Löyly

After Lumi had been put to bed, Aiti and I tossed the dishwater outside, each of us holding a handle, swinging it out onto the ground. We were just in time to see Einar streak out from the sauna to pump another bucket of water.

"Sadie, don't look," Aiti said, but out of a tangle of salt-and-pepper hair Einar's tube swung wild like the hand of an enthusiastic student.

Isa called him back to the sauna. "Einar, the ladies!"

Einar raised the full bucket up in one hand. "But it is for the ladies."

By the time we passed them on the sauna path, the men were barefoot, but back in their dirty daytime clothes. It was the first time they'd covered themselves in front of me. Always, when I'd been the washer girl, I had scrubbed their bodies while they'd joked with me: *You missed a spot, Sadie. Oh, I'm real stinky here in my armpits. Want to smell?* I wondered if they even knew how to clean themselves, without a woman there. I pictured them sniffing each other and asking: *Did I get it all?* Or the stranger picture: scrubbing each other with the same quiet attention a girl would give them. Impossible, I decided, for a man to attend to another man that way. They'd probably come out dirtier than ever, bits of ash and bark in their hair, scratches all over their backs where their friend had hit them too hard with the birch branches of the *vihta*.

In the small changing room, Aiti and I removed our clothes and hung them on pegs. We opened and shut the door to the sauna room quickly, like children playing a door-slamming game. Inside, the rocks on the stove tick-ticked. Karl had no doubt stoked it right before they exited, even though he knew the girls liked it cooler. Only men competed to prove who could handle the most. They must have laughed, imagining us walking in, the woodstove nearly rocking on its cast iron legs, the smokestack ready to take the skin off anyone who got too close.

The wooden boards had a touch that was almost a burn, but not quite. I didn't mind it. All we could do at first was breathe, lying on the pine benches to stay below the worst heat. Last light of evening transformed the outlines of the trees into etchings. Birds, so loud all summer, grew quiet earlier now, and all we heard was the iron ticking, beginning to calm down.

I looked at Aiti's body. She had let it relax, breasts lying flat on her chest, her shoulders down, her knees bent like a girl lazing on the grass, eyes closed. She seemed like a whole, untethered being, unburdened by objects calling her: dish, broom, soap, kettle. She had shed her daytime life, my naked mother.

"*Löyly?*" I asked, and she nodded.

"Not too much."

Einar's water bucket sat in the corner. I poured a dipperful on to the granite rocks and they yelled back at me, a high hiss that sounded dangerous; a few seconds later, they turned the water into steam. Aiti wrung out wet cloths for us to breathe through, to protect our lungs, and we waited for that blast of heat. After the steam receded, the sweat broke through our hot paper skins.

"Hoo," Aiti said. "That was a good one."

She'd birthed and nursed four children. Because the sauna was the cleanest, warmest place on any Finnish homestead, all of us except Karl had been born in this room. He emerged in the boarding house sauna, and Aiti frequently blamed his bad behavior on the questionable atmosphere of his birthplace.

I had tried to come out backwards, not headfirst the way babies are meant to. Aiti said I was too comfortable and lazy to come out the right way. They had to call in an English nurse from town, who turned me by pressing down hard on my mother's belly. "Her hands," Aiti said, and demonstrated on her naked body. "First here, then here. Like magic, Sadie, she moved you." I was named after this nurse with the magic hands.

I was the first to give in, to need air. Aiti said she'd come too, and so we barefooted out onto the front step. Aiti carried Einar's full water bucket, now warm, and used the wooden ladle, its curve scooped from a huge tree knot, to pour water over me. Normally, she'd be quick about it, but tonight she left her hand on my shoulder and took her time rinsing the sweat from my hair. Above our heads, the shape of the swan shone bright against the deep of the sky. Mummo told me once that the stars inside the swan's body made a cross, but Aiti said, "No, no. See those stars, her wings? She's a beautiful bird, she's *joutsen*." A small wind played over my wet skin. I felt like a child again, Lumi's age.

"You know that old story, where the young man, he get so crazy for needing a woman he run a sleigh cross the snow, roll her up in a big fur rug, throw her in a sled? Steal her away from her family? That," Aiti said, "still happens."

We sat on a board balanced on two stumps, our extra heat radiating skyward.

"Karl needs girlfriend. Maybe soon he gonna get one. Maybe not. Either way, you don't worry 'bout him no more. We strangle him, he does that to you again." She poured one last ladle of water over her own head and let it stream down her face as she stared out into the darkness. "But he not the only boy in the world. They all gonna come at you, Sadie, take what you got, you don't stop them.

"They gonna do *this*." She grabbed one of my breasts and squeezed hard. "This how they think."

When I stood up so did she, insisting, "They gonna do this," and she seized my wet hair and pressed her body against mine. "Lotta men don't mind," she said, her wiry underhair scratching my bare skin. "You think this is yours?" she asked, her right hand pinching and slapping at my rear.

"Quit! *Lopeta!*" I said, snot bubbling from my nose.

"Good, good," she said. "Yes. Fight me, Sadie," and she poked a hard finger into my belly, mocking. "Somebody does this to you, all you gonna do is cry?"

I had never hit my mother before, never yelled at or hated her, but that night I did all those things. Kicked her, clawed at her face, twisted my head away until I was free, which was when *she* began to cry. Her tears braided with the water from her dripping hair and fell down the broad bones and hollows of her face. She had scratches on her cheek and hands, and the next morning she would appear at breakfast with dark blue bruises all over her legs. I was so confused, so angry, though when she asked me to, I followed her back into the sauna, and curled on the lowest bench, away from her, she on the top one, amid the greatest heat. We both looked at the ceiling while she talked.

"My mother, she never tell me nothing. I go around thinking all men they good and sweet like your father. After he leave for America, I walk around town dreaming, dreaming, writing him letters, reading again and again the letters he send. That's all I got in my head, this love, and I go to the church just to sing, my heart is so full. I am the loudest singer in the bunch. We got a new pastor: beautiful family, young children, pretty wife. When he talk about Jesus, it like he himself fills up with heaven. One day he ask me stay after church, help with Easter flowers, such a holy man.

"He bring me up the stairs, to his office. Shut the door, and he grab me just like I grab you, Sadie. He push me against the door, shove his hand up my skirt, pull down his pants. I watch the wooden cross behind him on the wall, and all I can think is *This is a man of God?*

"He get done, he wipe my tears with his sleeve. He says, 'You go to America soon, Kata,' his breath like moldy cheese. 'Your husband, he can thank me later. I get you ready for him.'

"He ask me then, do I want to meet again before I sail away? He laughs when I shake my head no, says, 'Lost your voice, eh?'

"I never say nothing, Sadie. Not to *nobody*. After I leave the church, I walk to the sea, walk right in with all my clothes, and I stand there, almost freeze to death. I think maybe I let the cold take me, sink down with the cod and the eels, but then I think, Aarne's in America waiting for me, he want to build a house, start a family, and so I decide I won't die." Aiti's hands lay folded on her belly. "No matter what they do, Sadie, you don't let them kill you."

6.
Warren Gamaliel Harding

The rest of that long August we sweat in our clothes, drank dust, found the deep holes in the creek in the mid-afternoon, and walked it seemed whole days in fields of black-eyed Susan, grasshopper and bee, dry weed and heat-stilled bird. "Warren Gamaliel Harding."

When Isa said the president's name, extra rolls on the R's, it sounded almost obscene. Harding was always in some sort of trouble with my father. He'd run on a slogan of "less government in business, more business in government," which in Isa's eyes might as well have been translated as "more foxes in the hen house."

"What he does now?" My mother was all ears for this political talk. When she was in a boasting mood, she'd remind people that Finnish women had the right to vote *and* to run for office—"The first in the world!"—in 1906. That she'd missed this opportunity herself, arriving in America in 1905, mattered little. Of all the rotten things that happened in her home country, this was one point of pride she wouldn't deny herself.

"Well, he died," Isa said. "Heart attack in California. That's one good thing."

Sunday, the men sat reading the papers—*Industrialisti* out of Duluth, *Työmies* (*The Worker*) out of Superior,

Wisconsin—and smoking their sweet pipes. Though Einar was more interested in coffee and conversation, Isa took his reading time seriously. It was his chance to dive away from the family noise and be, as he said, with the men of the world, the great thinkers, in the realm of ideas. Aiti, because she never could do just one thing and call it good, managed our supper preparations while fitting me for a new dress. She'd ordered the fabric, a grade thicker and finer than our usual, when I started work and she was proud, as she always was, of her seamstress skills. *You won't find anything like this*, she said, *in those stores. Made for anybody.*

Einar tried and failed to pull my father from his deliberations, but found audience with the rest of us, at least. "Your Isa tell you about the ghost fish?" he said, looking at me, frozen where I was, but obviously fishing for Lumi, who took the whole bait without hesitation. She moved in close and he opened one long arm for her to nestle into.

"You know the Milford Mine is not really the Milford Mine," he said, and Lumi shook her head, though I guess we all knew the mine's history well enough, even her. "She used to be the Ida Mae, named after the hoity-toity wife of the East Coast owner. But then the lady died, didn't she, and with the man lost to grief, the mine fell to ruin…"

Isa interjected with a skeptical clearing of his throat, but didn't raise his eyes from the paper, so Einar continued. "The whole claim was abandoned, and slowly, slowly, the drifts filled with water.

"Lumi, you know about the underground rivers?" She shook her head. "Right under your feet RIGHT NOW," he said, and she climbed up on his knee, apparently unnerved by the possibility that our floorboards might be washed out from under us. "You see all the water in the lakes, sure, and in the swamps. But it doesn't stay there, no, no. It moves where it wants. Like a woman!"

He gave Aiti a side-eye. She was usually good for an argument when he made his bold statements about womankind but, like Isa, she resisted. "So the fish moved in. Your northern pike, your walleye. Even crappies, and those sunfish you like, Lumi. And perch!" He tickled her like a swarm of minnows and she laughed, delighted. "All where your Isa and me, and your brother Karl, where all the men work. That was their new home, I guess, till the new owner, he pumped out all that water, and all the fish with it, back into the lake. And they gave the mine a new name, Milford, and we got us a job. But those fish, I seen them, Lumi, I swear to God. Sometimes they bump into you, confused about what people are doing down there, like the water is still everywhere, and the air we breathe just a dream."

Aiti's pins entered my waistband in such quick succession I feared she'd be three pins ahead before she noticed any piercing of my skin. I pulled my stomach away from the fabric but Aiti told me to hold still and shook me for good measure. "You sway like *koivu*," she said, like a birch.

"You know, it's bad luck to change a name." Einar was looking for more than Lumi's ears this time. "Can't hide what happened before. It stays. All that bad news, that time of no money. All those ghost fish." Lumi took on the role of nibbling fish this time, her hands making a meal of Einar's ears and high forehead. "I shoulda quit when they changed names."

"There!" Aiti said. Her mouth full of pins, she admired the fit, drawing her hands down my sides as though I were a sculpture she'd made. The dress would be done in one shot, with no waste, no ripping and redoing of seams.

"It's too tight," I said, feeling exposed and suddenly sick to my stomach.

She only shook her head and smiled. "Like sealskin," she said. "Made only for you."

Einar looked at me for a minute like I was a stranger. "Hmmmph. Kata, Aarne, you got a young lady on your hands." He whistled. "Nothing but trouble, hey. Those young girls." He reached deep into one of his trouser pockets and pulled out a wrinkled piece of paper. "Which reminds me. Aarne, listen to this:

__Dreaming of Oulu, and You__

Fit prosperous bachelor Suomi. Good job. Own home. Chickens. Educated. Friendly. Seeks young beautiful Suomi woman, age not important but should have permission to marry. Sun-kissed cheeks, happy smile, good temper important. Dancing okay. Girl who hates big city. Likes ponds and snow, warm fire, laughing at jokes. Farmer's daughter okay. Fisher daughter okay. Worker daughter of some kind. Our life could start right now! Waiting for your picture."

* * *

A little sheepish, he added, "I got help with the words."

"Fit?" Isa asked. Einar sucked in his gut and patted it.

"Prosperous?" asked Aiti.

"Save all my money by eating at your house!" Einar said.

"Young beautiful girl?" Isa stared over his paper, his reading glasses giving him the look of a teacher. "What girl gonna come here for that face you got?"

Aiti followed. "She asks for picture, what you send?"

Einar carefully pulled out his wallet, and from a sleeve of new paperboard drew a photograph and handed it to my mother, who stared in disbelief.

"Who?"

"Let me see that, Kata," Isa said. She perched on the arm of his chair and shared the photo, Lumi peering through a small window in their bodies so she could see too.

"Einar..." Isa said.

"What?"

"If this is you, you are eighteen years old, no more," Isa said.

I moved to take a look. Young Einar had lots of slicked back hair, bright eyes, pressed jacket and shirt. He appeared not much older than me, full of promise, full of mischief.

"Not so long ago," Einar said, to a chorus of scoffs. "Haven't changed so much." To which he got double.

Aiti handed back the photo, which Einar retrieved and put back in his wallet with exaggerated care. "Some friends you are."

"What about Judy?" Aiti asked.

Einar huffed. "Judy puts me last. Got ricing to do, that's two weeks gone. Some little cousin got a toothache, she gotta mix up medicine. That might take one week. Maybe it's time to harvest fish. Or berries. Or she got something else going on. What about Einar? When is Einar time?" He grumbled, it seemed, mostly to himself, an old argument. "Whenever Judy says it's Einar time. That's it. I got no say."

It seemed kinder to let Einar grieve his present circumstances in silence, especially since no Finn girl, we were sure, would ever take his bait. Isa returned to his papers, I counted the minutes till I'd be released from the pin-filled dress, and Aiti checked on the Sunday dinner. She had time for her own thoughts, though, and soon spoke up.

"Aarne, how long that liquor gonna be in our barn?"

At first Isa appeared not to hear her, or to be ignoring her on purpose, but he flipped the pages once, twice, and then said, as if it had nothing to do with her question, "Been a murder last week. Just off the mine. They say the man he was running whiskey."

Kata banged a few pots but didn't speak.

Isa cleared his throat. "It's maybe a little dangerous right now."

"What you going to do then, Aarne? Throw it on the ground?"

"I'm just saying, Kata. Got to sit on it awhile, maybe. Let everything cool down."

Einar shuffled his paper, unworried. "Or I call Judy, see what she can do."

"It's more dangerous for her. You know that, Einar."

Einar shrugged. "Judy knows people, people who know people. Not so hard for her. Think she minds lying to the alcohol cops? I don't think so. Remember, she's an actress."

The room briefly filled with what seemed a respectful silence, then Isa nodded. He looked only at Aiti when he spoke.

"Maybe it's easier to bring it that way, through her village. You stick with people you know, Kata, to do this sort of thing. It doesn't hurt anybody that way. Nobody gets hurt."

* * *

Judy was sent to the Cross Lake School, up on Red Lake Reservation, when she was only four. Funny, she said, because the government called them the Non-Removable Mille Lacs Band of Ojibwe, after her people helped white settlers during the Dakota War. That school cut her hair, burned her clothes, kept her away from everyone she loved. She told stories of blowing lye bubbles, soap the punishment for speaking her own language. Long ruler laid across the hands her punishment for crying. Children died in the dormitory from typhus, from dysentery. She ran from there so fast, she said, her hair grew back all in one day and she'd never cut it again.

"You're so proud of that, Einar," Aiti said. "You know a girl who lies."

My ears burned.

"Not lying, Kata. An art."

"Dress up fancy, put on makeup, pretend to be person you are not. I don't see good thing there." She bent over to rearrange the pots in the cupboard, loud enough so no one could hear themselves talk till she was done. "Enough work in this world without play," she said. "Grown woman should know better."

Judy would have come back home, but a sheriff's posse had burned her village in 1911, forcibly removed the people of Chief Wadena so developers could take the land. So when a Pathé Western film director and his Winnebago girlfriend came through Minnesota looking for native actors, she followed them to California.

"But Shakespeare, Kata. Don't you think?" Einar said. "People need to laugh and cry about something not their own life."

"Enough in this life," she said. "No point looking at it, when you got to go home and live it too. Better to know what is evil, what is wrong in this world, make yourself tough. Go cry at play? Send you home softer, life no easier. What is point of that?"

In the pictures Judy was White Cloud, a Sioux princess. Died a thousand times at the hands of fake cowboys, gave wise warnings, stirred a cast-iron pot. She even met Wild Bill before he died. Played cards with him and won.

"You don't believe in change, Kata."

"Ha," she said. "I see what you call change. Leave country. Leave family. Leave your words on the other side of the ocean. What changes for me? Still house to keep. Children and man to feed. Change is no picnic."

We all looked at each other. Where had she picked up an American phrase like that?

"Your English, Kata. Getting better!"

"No thanks to anybody else. Only me," she said. "Meet up with the other Suomi ladies, we figure it out. Nobody cares if we know nothing. All of you go out, learn English, keep it to yourself. Let the mother sit at home, work, work…" She switched to Finnish as she stomped out of the room, still talking a mean streak.

* * *

My parents' small picture sat in a frame on the nice piece of furniture, the one with the wooden face carved in curls, the one where Aiti kept the good sheets for company, embroidered with blue and orange flowers, tangled up with small spear-shaped leaves. In the picture, she has just gotten to America. They have just been married. She wears the white high-necked dress she packed in her chest. I always pictured her like me, early, before anything could happen to her. To know now that she'd thought of dying already, that she'd almost drowned in the bay they called *Kempeleenlahti*, the one she'd grown up hearing every day and night from her parents' cabin on the farm outside Niemenranta. I couldn't believe that, at sixteen, she'd been so ready to join the water.

I knew her serious smile better than my own, her lips pressed tight together, just the smallest upturn at each corner. Her eyes a deep piercing brown. We'd always laughed that Aiti seemed to be mad at the photographer. We pictured him safe behind the box camera and still frightened by the accusation in her stare.

She was so beautiful. Her skin immaculate and smooth, her hair shining and luxurious even pulled back from her face and braided in a crown. How my father must have wanted to unpin it. I didn't like to think too long on the rest of their wedding night, but I could picture the way he must have held his breath before he let loose her hair from its confinement, when he brushed the back of his hand against its length to feel its softness.

And Isa. Aarne Marttila, twenty-seven years old. Eleven years her elder. He must have thought her such an innocent. A Finn girl raised far from the boardinghouse saloons, from the whiskey, cards, and rough jokes of men.

Maybe Aiti thought her stories would make me stronger, but the whole world seemed dangerous to me now in a way it hadn't quite before. Filled with preachers, brothers, liquor runners, thieves. I felt more exposed. The thought of my new dress against my skin made me sweat and I hated to think of the stares. People I knew all of a sudden seeing me as something new, a growing, ripening thing. I pictured myself putrid as a bruised peach, flies everywhere, juice seeping.

* * *

I found the playing card one Sunday when I swept under Karl's bed. On the back, a photograph of a girl astride a dappled stallion. The card was well-handled and bent at all its edges, the shine dulled off all but the horse's rear. The young woman, who knows how old, looked into the camera. She didn't smile, but neither did she look surprised. She was herself, sitting stolidly on her own haunches. Unlike me, she didn't curve her shoulders over to hide her chest. Instead, she sat straight up, unapologetic, as the thin straps of her lace chemise fell down her arms, exposing her breasts, soft small moons, moonshadowed. The lacework was good, the kind Aiti's mother was known for: her quick hands by candlelight summoning fish and flower, linden and star from twisted thread. The girl in the photo wore braided lace. It looked like water, the way it moved, tangled streams that unite and divide after a long spring rain.

    Where Karl got the card, I could guess. Those miners must have lots of them, though their grubby hands would ruin them. Maybe they kept them close to their hearts while they worked, or in their lunch pails hidden in a slit under the tacked gingham lining. Who knows what they secret away? How many girls each man needs to see, naked as though she were his. And what in this easy exposure excited more than the woman at home, her nightdress half-on, half-off. Maybe it was the act of stilling that motion, the capture of everyday beauty, which usually passed too quickly. Maybe all the men wanted was the time to stare at what they found beautiful, no matter the mood of the woman. I could hear the picture girl's silent thoughts as she was asked to hold still a few minutes longer, while the man ducked his head under the black coverlet to fiddle with knobs and lenses and adjusted the angle. And as he emerged breathing heavily, fussing like a schoolmarm with the lay of her shoulder strap, exposing the most affecting ratio of skin to fabric.

    I feared I would need to know these things eventually: to study what men loved, to pose without appearing to. To know, because I'd learned how, to present myself in the best light.

* * *

Bring out the cash, maybe a person could get what they want. Hand it over like it's nobody's business where it came from. They look at you, amazed. That family has money? That family trusts this girl with a hundred dollar bill? No. The fantasy always ended there. They'd call the police. They'd find my parents, say *your girl's a thief*. The little piece of paper would go in the government pocket and I'd never touch it again. But what use was it if I couldn't spend it? It was like having no money at all. Even worse than that. A poverty made clear and aching. Food behind a glass case. Riches in a safe.

The next Saturday I unfurled the stolen bill from its hiding place, gave it a kiss for luck, and smuggled it in my stockings to work. When Mrs. Kaminski went upstairs for a minute, Sam off with deliveries and the rest of the family above, I pressed the button to open the register, holding the cash drawer with my belly so its bell wouldn't ring. Saturdays were busy, all the miners' wives in with the weekly pay—the farmers and the other townsfolk too—and there were plenty of twenty-dollar bills. I took five, careful to double and triple check the number, and slipped my own bill underneath the remaining stack. With any luck, no one would notice. And this, at least, wasn't a crime. An equal exchange. Still, my cold hands shook as I closed it, just as quiet, just as neat, and said a prayer for my own protection.

I was feeling proud of myself till I realized even a twenty was an impossible amount in my possession. I risked it again, the same opening, the same switch of large for small, a twenty for a ten, five, and five ones, but this time my breath rang ragged in my ears. I wouldn't have heard an elephant on the stairs behind me and I didn't hear Celia until she stood in front of me, a quizzical expression on her face.

"Didn't think you had it in you, Mouse," she said.

7.
The Photographer's Bear

Doom in the stories I read came in a flash, all at once after a slow build. The main character flawed in a way that made her sin, in secret, at inopportune times, so that when judgment arrived it was like a vengeful Mummo angel dubiously in flight, heavy bones and padded flesh in a wool overcoat, *tsking* at you for doing wrong when you'd been raised right and knew better.

Celia, my present doom, was all angles in her trousers and button-down shirt, her freckles bright on her cheekbones.

"Are you running away?"

The squawk that left my mouth was animal: caught and desperate, just before the knife. My hands seemed to know better what to do, laying out the bills in order on the counter, marking on a scrap of paper the equation: $100 = $20, $20, $20, $20, $10, $5, $1, $1, $1, $1, $1. *Making change*, I wrote, and gestured wildly toward the open register, which I would not touch now for anything.

Celia dug deep in the drawer of large bills.

"On the bottom," I croaked.

She retrieved my stolen treasure and squinted at it under the lamp bulb. "It's real?"

I nodded.

"Where in the world does a girl like you get a hundred-dollar bill?" She seemed to be asking herself, or the universe, not me. "Are you a magician or a thief?"

"It's not mine," I said, and the admission intensified the heat in my face. "It's my mother's. She sold an old watch, gold from Finland. She needs the small bills. I thought it would be okay." I paused to see if my lie had any legs. "I'm sorry?" No response. "I should have asked."

"Are you sure some of it isn't for you?" Celia was giant and wise before me, a high court judge. "Listen here, isn't there something you want?"

Before I knew what I'd say, the words were out. "I want to be like you." And the second I said them, I knew they were true. "I want short hair. And pants."

Celia let out a low whistle. "Well, aren't you a surprise. Are you sure?"

I nodded.

"Then close that up, quick," she gestured toward the register, "and let's get out of here. I know just what to do."

She galloped up the stairs and exchanged loud words with her family. I waited the longest five minutes in history, sure I was about to face the wrath of my employers and be led away in handcuffs to spend the rest of my sorry life in the Crosby jail. Celia appeared, triumphant, and pushed an old leather purse into my hands.

"Put the money in here," she said. "You can't keep all that in your shoe."

I thought if she took pity on me she might shout "Run!" to give me a head start. And I'd live a fugitive life, me and my hundred dollars, hunted by shame.

But she wrapped one skinny arm around me and hustled me out the door. "We've got an excuse and the whole afternoon!" she said, and I followed her out, my feet floating above the sidewalk, a free criminal, a lying working girl, a Finn with money in her purse, more money than anyone could ever imagine or ever see again.

* * *

"So I figure your fee, as moneychanger, should be fifteen percent. That means, dear pupil, that you'll bring eighty-five dollars back to your mother, and keep your fee, fifteen dollars, for yourself. And I have five," she said, "from my allowance, so the movie will be my treat." Seeing my face, she laughed. "Don't look so shocked! You're a child. You're supposed to go to the movies."

I was so far gone at this point, so far past doing the right thing, I decided right then to go all to the bad. For one afternoon, at least. I heard myself saying aloud one of Karl's favorite outlaw sayings, *might as well be hanged for a sheep as a lamb.*

"Let's go to Paris!" Celia said. "*The Hunchback of Notre Dame* is playing." She paused to assess me. "But first we have to take care of this." She pulled the pins and ribbon from my hair, ran her fingers through my braids till they hung in a bumpy river down my back. "You're sure?"

When I said yes, she pulled me down the street and into the hair salon, Miss Kate's. On the wall, a poster of bobbed movie stars shouted "If You Must Do It Show This To Your Barber."

"So what'll it be? Dutch bob? Boyish bob? Permanently waved?" Celia turned to me. "You know, Bebe Daniels just pins her hair up in back so it looks like a bob. You don't have to cut it for real."

Miss Kate herself plopped me down in a chair and held my hair up below my ears. "Can you come back every week? You'd look fine in a water wave."

My feeling of being awash with money faded immediately. After today, I would be in jail—either in town or in the chicken coop, but either way I'd never be free again—so spending more money later was out of the question.

The hairdresser sighed. "Too bad. Then it's the Dutch bob for you. You'll have to comb out your bangs to take care of that cowlick you got. Okay? Okay." And off came my hair, a full foot of it. I felt the ghost of my mother's hands as each section fell to the floor: rinsing and combing, braiding and pinning. There'd be no more work for her to do now. I'd own my head, and care for it myself.

* * *

The sweaters in Randall's Boutique fell halfway to my knees. Thick cable-knit, dead-leaf brown shot through with green. For the first time since my leg bones began to lengthen, and my hideous chest to sprout, I felt covered. In the mirror, the curves of my body were safely hidden inside the long yarn rectangle. Only the bottom foot of my skirt moved: a dark brown plaid kicking out past my knees, twirling over thick woolen tights. This would be my uniform. No more gathered waists. No more buttoned bosoms. I'd be an armored Joan of Arc.

Celia held my work dress, which appeared nothing but rags to me now, part of an old life which had nothing to do with me. She began to fold it, but I said no, put it in the trash. Nobody could weave my hair back on my head, or persuade me to wear that dress again.

* * *

It was Celia's idea to get the photo taken. A keepsake, she said, of this momentous day of change. I thought a picture was frivolous—and, I admit, I was afraid to leave evidence of my crimes, though of course they'd be obvious to everyone soon enough—but she insisted. "My treat," she said.

The photographer's studio was tucked down a back alley behind the tannery. The air stank of skins and harsh chemicals, tall stacks of new leather with no chance to breathe. On the red-lacquered door a sign, *Samuel S. Swenson*, PHOTOGRAPHER. *Open every day. Sundays 1:30–3:30 pm.*

A bright bell announced our arrival as we descended a short flight of stairs to a dim and quiet basement, and after a moment a large head emerged from behind a black velvet curtain. I was afraid he might find two young girls ridiculous, but he only nodded when Celia told him our business.

"Mademoiselles," he said, bowing so we could see the coffee can–sized bald patch on his large head, his stocky arms sheathed to the elbows by rubber gloves. "I serve at your pleasure. Make yourselves at home while I finish up."

Propped in one corner, though seeming to preside over the whole studio, stood a great black bear. His teeth as long as my hand. The claws each a blade Karl would envy. The tongue a pink roast Aiti might steal for her oven. Lumi, of course, would want to take it home. To pet its silky black pelt, pull its small ears. You could embrace this one, stuffed and silent, without fear, though its teeth and claws held menace. The span of its mouth yawned dangerously large. And its eyes were so small there'd be no chance of mercy. It would devour you before it even knew who you were.

The slimness of its body, standing up, was nearly human. If a man and a bear walked in the woods when the light was low, maybe it would take you a minute to tell the difference. Its ears set to the side like the rim of a man's fedora, its arms hanging from the soft slop of its shoulders like any man in town out for a stroll.

Only when you got too close would you say to yourself: that wet nose is not so human. Those jacket and pants made of fur. That smile not so welcoming as it looked from far away.

Mr. Swenson emerged after a few minutes, his gloves and apron gone, wearing a faded but well-made suit. He arranged us on a wooden bench padded with sheepskin and hid his face behind a camera covered with black cloth, so all we could see was the dark face of the lens. His large body, bent over like that, was comical, like another bear playing hide-and-seek. Celia and I held our bodies still in pretend nonchalance. I'm sure I was scowling, because suddenly all I could think was this was the picture they'd use in the papers when the cops scooped me up and brought me to jail.

He fussed with levers and gears, his breath loud and labored, then stood up, his shoulders hunched up near his ears. "No, no. Not like that. Would you permit me?" He moved closer, studied us through a rectangle made with his two hands. Then he used a long pointer, the kind our teachers kept by the blackboard, to lift up Celia's shoe until one leg crossed over the other. And the end of the pointer then, deft as a mother's hand, tucked one raft of my new bangs behind my ear. We laughed at the trick, though I could just as easily have gasped. There was something intimate, something strange, about his actions, though he hadn't, himself, touched us.

Still he remained unsatisfied with what he saw through the camera. "You girls are too serious," he said. "Like old maids. Let's try something different."

At the bear's feet sat a pirate chest, its leather hinges frayed almost to the point of breaking. Swenson carefully opened its lid and leaned it against the bear's knees. He drew out a silver-sequined dress and held it in front of his body, which made us laugh.

"You're modern girls. Flappers?" He moved, surprisingly quick for such a large man, to the opposite wall, where he revealed one of a stack of painted backdrops: a city of lights and a blue-lit jazz club, colorful caricatures of glamorous, bare-legged women and tuxedoed men dancing and drooping over round tables with drinks in their hands.

Celia leaned close. "Want to?"

"Why not?" I said. What, after all, would it matter, after everything I'd already done.

"I will retire," Swenson said, with a dramatic flourish of his arms, "to the gentleman's room while you change."

I put on the silver dress and Celia wore a red one, a deep V in the front showing absolutely nothing, a cheroot in her hand and a black feather boa that looked like a strangled turkey around her neck. Swenson's chest held strappy shoes and costume jewelry. We took some of everything. Even though I'd spent the whole day covering myself, dressing up with Celia felt delicious. Because this wasn't real. We weren't in public. Just us and the camera, so we could pretend to be anything.

Swenson seemed excited by our choices and quickly took five or six pictures.

"What's this going to cost?" I asked, remembering that we'd come in for just one and now we'd gone far past that.

"For you girls, these extras are free," he said. "I'll charge you for only one."

So we were flappers, and then cowboys, mountain peaks rising behind our lonely range. After that we were in Egypt—Celia as Cleopatra and me as Marc Antony—by the Sphinx. Our voices cracked from too much laughter, Swenson spurring us to more and more expansive postures.

"I have time," Swenson said. "Do you want to do more?"

But it was time for the movie, so the photographer withdrew and we returned to our normal selves. I was dizzy with the changes, trying on so many lives in one day.

"Come back in a week. I'll have the best ones ready. And if money is a concern," he said, his abnormally small, abnormally white teeth fully bared, "there are ways to get that."

We ran all the way to the movie theater, not caring if the speed of our pounding feet flustered respectable men and women on the wooden sidewalk. We bought our tickets and flopped down in seats right in front just as the projector lit the screen.

But before we could embrace poor Quasimodo—his curved back and unbalanced body, his love for Esmeralda the gypsy, his bells—Pathé flooded us with news. In black and white, in curly script, *The Japanese Earthquake: Graphic pictures that tell their own story of greatest catastrophe in the World's History!* 150,000 dead in Tokio. The buildings shaken to the ground. Refugees chased from the city by fire. As they listed the damage in each city, buildings burned, people killed, they played footage from happier days. A boy my age carried a baby on his back. A child held her parents' hands down a busy street. Men with Western hats. Old ladies with elaborately piled hair. Colorful banners waving from shops, bobbing parasols. Then more recent photos: piles of burned-out Fords. A hollowed bookstore. A ruined sumo wrestling arena.

The tsunami rose from the placid horizon of the sea and took down every small perfect house. You could see half-porches covered by pitched eaves, pillars and doors, balanced and lovely by the sea, homes with views of everything: fishermen, sunrise, mountains too. They said it had been hundreds of years since the sea rose up angry enough to sweep the land of its people. What had they done? Whose prayers were less than perfect and was it just a day or decades of half-hearted communications that decided their fate? Mummo would surely have an opinion on that.

It looked like one of Lumi's playthings, the way a house bobbed along the chaotic rush of water, only its roof showing, a small dog riding on top. Boats on their sides, floating rafts of horses and cattle. Mats of debris pressed against obstacles, piling higher and higher, and still the water moved through it all without impediment.

8.
Miss X

If I expected a scene, I didn't get one. My family bought my lies. That the Kaminski girls had cut my hair and gifted me their extra clothes. That they had piles and piles of things they'd outgrown, given to them in an unending stream by rich relatives in St. Paul. Of course I didn't mention the photography session. I almost let slip that I'd been to the movies, but caught myself just in time. And the money? All those bills were too big now for their old hiding place, so I rolled them into a tight cigar and sewed them into the hem of my new dress.

Though it had been nothing but hot dust all August, when September hit and school began the dogwoods turned deep red and purple overnight. The men left while the grass was frosted and the moon and stars were out. I was glad I didn't need to leave so early, although the sound of their boots on the cold ground was fresh and crisp. I imagined silent film bank robbers tip-toeing away from a heist. The air was still cold when Lumi and I walked to school, so cold the bumblebees slept in the night-folded asters and both were covered with dew. Lumi blew on them to wake them with her breath. She loved when wild creatures were hurt or, like the bees, stunned by the cold. It gave her a chance to catch up with them, to carry and pet them, as if they belonged to her. She sang the bumblebees a little song and would've taken one to school if I hadn't put an end to it. "They'll sting you when they wake."

She shook her head. "No, they'd know I was a kind master." But she left the bees where they slept.

We only had to walk halfway to school: through the woods on a deer path till we met the road, where the bus picked us up. After a summer of solitude, mushrooms grew up everywhere from the leaf layers. With their fragile stalks and fluted gills, they seemed too delicate to put themselves in traffic, but they seemed to prefer the paths that people and animals took. It wasn't as if they were made of rubber, strong enough to spring back from a boot, a hoof, a tire. The easiest things in the world to break. Kids did it accidentally all the time, even when they were just trying to look closer. I'd always said a little apology when my hands were clumsier than I wanted them to be. The puffballs, though, you almost didn't feel bad squishing them. Meant to be popped, asking for it. No root to feel bad about. Roll it, toss it. And then, when they were ready—dry and filled with whatever they were filled with—to stomp with all your might, letting their insides out into the air. You didn't feel bad because you were helping. The bumpy white ball didn't exist anymore, but it lived in the larger sense, didn't it? Millions of spores thrown out to the world, to make millions more puffballs for new children.

* * *

After school we had our first play practice with Miss X. Her family were lake people, Celia had said. A term I hated, as though they owned the lakes when we were the ones who lived here year-round and saw the water with all its faces. But it did feel like theirs when the weather finally turned and the buds came out, the peepers sang in the ice-free ponds and the birds too, when the sun gave us its favor and the world again felt welcoming instead of hostile. That first good weekend, the lake people were sure to show up, inhabit their cottages, fill the roads with cars and the stores with business, the ring of the cash register, and the "Add that too. And another of those, thanks." Money no object, which was already clear, because who but the rich could afford to keep two houses, one just for play. One just for sunny days and weekends, just for boats and frankfurters. I tried to think of other names so they would lose their claim. Cottage people? Weekend people? Something that would taint them a bit, counter their obvious power and freedom, both of which I'm sure I wanted, if only to try on like department store dresses, to see how they looked on me.

We didn't mix much with them, though we served them. It was strange to have a lake person as a teacher, though I thought of Miss X as a city person. She was marked more by her exposure to art and philosophy, to the fashion and theatre of Chicago, than any connection to or ownership of our town. She seemed unmoored by any allegiances here, seemed not to care what people thought of her rinsed-red unbound hair, her silk stockings, her lack of polite convention. She wouldn't smile when you expected her to. Didn't defer to the powerful. Didn't make nice or agree. Which made everyone else uncomfortable. And which reminded me how often I *did* do those things, to disappear, to get along.

It didn't seem like she came from typical lake people, though, those pinstripe-suited businessmen and well-bred society wives. She wouldn't bring marshmallow delight to the town picnic. Miss X was the child of artists: a writer, an actress. Her father famous for some book he wrote about pioneer days in southern Minnesota, the hardships of the working man. Isa had read it and given it grudging praise, though the author wasn't a Finn. The mother, a star in her day, was painted, it was rumored, in little more than her bathrobe by more than one well-known scoundrel, though she was not the famous Madame that John Singer Sargent had painted, the one from which Miss X took her name. Both parents must have brought in enough money to buy the house on the lake, if not the respectability that usually went with it.

After a day of classes, it felt strange to stay in the empty school. The new building so cavernous, five stories of sprawling brick and glass, more at home in the city than here on the Cuyuna Range. *That's where our wages go*, Isa said. *Bosses make so much they can afford to show off, look generous with monuments to themselves.* He seemed pleased at least that his children would benefit, even though he and his fellow workers would not.

It was a big production, and there were a good two dozen of us swarming the empty stage. Marvelous pulled me into the dressing room, where the girls played with powder and blush. We played at wild girls, dropped costume dresses off our shoulders, made our faces into paintings. We walked onto the stage, experiments in disarray.

In a back corner, a tall boy sat on a metal stool, open buckets at his feet, a bandana tucked into the back pocket of his paint-spattered trousers. I stared so hard I forgot to pick up my feet, and tripped and fell to my knees. While I had emerged in costume feeling large and protected, as the painter boy turned and noticed me I was immediately brought down to size. He smiled at me as if he knew everything about me and found it amusing. How horrifying:

one minute to be crossing the stage, following Marvelous, worried about what the director would ask me to do, and the next moment to be hit with eyes.

What an odd boy, to stare and not say anything. To smile at me strangely as if he were making fun of me. As if I was asking him to look at me and not just minding my own business.

Shouldn't a painter be painting? Shouldn't he control those eyes? The worst kind of rudeness to unleash them in my direction when I was so clearly an easy mark. I scowled at him and found my feet with as much dignity as I could, hoping he would forget me.

Miss X swooped in from the wings, only five feet tall but with far greater impact. Her hair, an exuberant cloud of scarlet curls, was held back from her forehead by a silver satin scarf.

"All right, people! We have so little time! Girls, to center stage please. Chat later.

Where are the boys? What kind of trouble can we make without boys? Ah, of course….sprawling in the paid seats," she said. "Up! Now!

"The set is not yet painted, but picture, actors and actresses, the scene. The hills of Greece. The Parthenon! Olive trees. Grapes ripening in the sun. Breezes from the Aegean Sea. Picture fishermen, tanned and glistening on their whitewashed boats, throwing their nets, bringing up fish and squid.

"Why do the women go wild? That is the question! But. Perhaps you girls know the answer. Have you ever glimpsed a boy golden as the sun? So beautiful you think he must be a god?"

All the girls tittered and rustled their dresses, shifted on our feet, embarrassed. The boys cleared their throats miserably

"You know the Pied Piper? Dionysus is like that. He's the song and the call they've been waiting for all their lives. He pours the wine. He brings them to the hills. He gives them a dream. Now, children! Dance like you know what that feels like."

This was an unfortunately brisk start to the world of theatre for most of us, country children with no real experience. A few groans escaped the pack, but no one moved.

"I thought we were supposed to be angels," Marvelous said. "Wrapped in white. Barefoot angels."

Celia nodded in agreement. "He's God, right? We're his angels."

Miss X raised her chest like a proud bird. "All of you. Be still. Watch!" She clapped her hands and moved downstage center, facing the audience. She bent over an imaginary washbasin, scrubbing and wringing clothes, her countenance morose. Then she looked up, astonished and youthful. Her eyes tracked something going by and she let go the invisible washing and tripped over herself leaving the site of her work. Her blind walking became, as she moved across the stage, a subtle, then fervent hip shaking. She punched her hands at the sky.

"Girls! Come now! Join me. Boys, turn your backs." We girls arranged ourselves like ducklings behind Miss X. The boys formed a line facing away from the empty seats. "See how I'm moving? Do this."

We giggled, nervous, our heads bent toward the ground, until Marvelous stepped out in front, tied a knot in her skirt to show some leg, and began to shake first one hip then the other. The rest of us laughed and one by one we joined the group downstage, dancing.

Marvelous mimed taking a long pull from a bottle and passed it to me. I took a swig myself and felt a thrill from the imaginary liquor. Pretty soon all of us were full of whatever intoxicant Miss X had unleashed on the stage. We knew the boys were there, that they could hear the way our feet fell to the music, could hear the swish of our skirts and the clap of our bare hands. We looked at the backs of their legs, shoulders, necks and heads as we danced, and wondered just what they were thinking.

Miss X called out, "Dionysus!"

From the wings strode a man, not old but too old to be a student, holding an ivy-topped staff. His chest was bare save for an animal skin draped across one shoulder, and his hair fell in a wig of beaded braids down his back.

"Leader of our dance," Miss X said, her voice low and urgent. "The ground there flows with milk and flows with wine and flows with honey from the bees. Fragrant as the Syrian frankincense, the pine fumes from the torch our spellbound leader holds high."

Miss X let the boys turn around and asked us all to lie down on the stage. She and Dionysus walked back and forth, weaving between our prone bodies, telling us about their time in the Chicago Little Theatre. About spending time out East with the Provincetown Players. Meeting Eugene O'Neill, Edna St. Vincent Millay: *We were very tired, we were very merry—We had gone back and forth all night on the ferry. It was bare and bright, and smelled like a stable—But we looked into a fire, we leaned across a table, We lay on a hill-top underneath the moon; And the whistles kept blowing, and the dawn came soon.*

Listening to her recitation brought us there too. *Yes*, I said to the ferry. *Yes* to the apples and pears, *yes* to the shawl-covered lady and the hill-top under the moon.

"Soon the bacchanalian girl will be full of happiness and gambols," Miss X said, reading from the play. "Lightfooted as a filly 'round its mother in the pastures."

9.
The Painter

Over the next two weeks, the boy painted more sky. He painted hills. He gave olives to the olive trees, deep fleece to the sheep. Through an open palace of pillars you could see a town of white buildings with orange roofs, pretty in the distance. I thought of the beautiful walk you could take if you could just enter the scene.

On stage was a toga-wrapped Marvelous, bare-shouldered, the fabric following her curves, her tender skin surely calling to everyone. She threw a hand across her forehead, leaned back and sighed. "Oh, my love! Where can you be? My love has gone a'foraging."

"No, no. Voyaging, not foraging," said Miss X.

Marvelous frowned, clearly unconvinced. She gestured to the sheep.

"He is at sea." Miss X pointed at the painted bit of blue wave at the edge of the panorama. "Out there. The world is not only pasture."

"My love has gone a'voyaging," Marvelous said, and began to sob.

The painter appeared at my side and threw a warm, heavy arm across my shoulder, which shrank away as quickly as it could, though it remained trapped. "How's she doing?"

"Well."

"Well, what?"

"No, she's doing well. Fine. She's marvelous," I said, and I meant it.

The painter laughed. "You're a fan, huh?" He put a hand to his forehead. "I think she hams it up too much."

The armpits of a boy you like smell different than, say, the armpit of one's brother or father, neighbor or grandfather. Even if, like the painter's, they smell overripe, somewhat bitter, something else perks up your nose in interest. Something like musk, something animal, something fur. I could picture it under his shirt, the bare skin leading away in several directions. Ridiculously, I imagined placing small kisses like deer trails across his skin, working away from the too-strong scent, but the air still perfumed around my head. How to live in this embarrassing body, subject to the whims of one's nose, the armpits of a boy? I moved away.

Miss X seemed to know plenty about the body, about the ways people hide or show them. *Stop fussing with your hands*, she'd say. *Get them out of your pockets*. This, to the shy and inexperienced ones, including me. To the bold, like Marvelous, she said, *Stop gesticulating! Do you intend to slap your partner in the face? Are you Quixote's windmill? No one acts like that in real life. Calm down.*

When I thought I was showing real emotion on my face she said, *Are you a stone? Are you even alive? Look in the mirror until you understand what joy looks like.* To Marvelous, she said, *You are more gruesome than a carnival mask. Your version of mirth resembles the death throes of an especially hideous courtesan!*

* * *

To prove a point once during rehearsal, Miss X walked silently to the painter and ran her hands through his hair without asking. One swift and smooth motion, her fingers playing in a wave and back out again in a flash. Touch. When she turned on her ballet slippers and rejoined the troupe, everyone watched the economy of her hips under the silk of her dress. To be so in your body that you could call attention to yourself without words. I didn't know about that. The gulf between the way I lived in my body and the way she lived in hers seemed impassable. Be born elsewhere, to other people. My body was mine only in solitude, only with family, only in the sauna at the end of a long day, giving into the heat and the soft lamplight.

"Wonder is extraneous," she told us. "It's the appearance of wonder you want. Can it be read from the high seats? What does it take to be understood? You should know how your face looks in the mirror. You have a mirror, don't you? You don't rely on a still pond? You aren't swamp dwellers?" She paused for effect. "I didn't think so. I'm sure you Finns and Cornish game hens have some culture, however primitive. You don't have any rituals you can bring to the stage, do you? Anything wild? Anything Greek?"

In rehearsals I blended in best I could, alternately bold and stubbornly shy, hoping not to be noticed, but still she found me out.

"You're a mute thing. I've heard you sing, behind the others. You'll do it then, just enough. The tiniest stream of air from between your lips. Hunched over roadside weed, that's how you read, up close and far away. Goldenrod, bending her head in a field of goldenrod. That's what you are." Miss X sighed. "You might as well go blend in over there with the others, since that's what you do best. Go, go! I don't have time to spend giving confidence to those who won't take it."

* * *

"*I'm bored with you*, is what she said." Lumi sprawled half-off, half-on the bed, her bare feet tapping the floor.

"Don't play with her then."

"And then she told on me that I put dirt on the slide."

"Play with someone nicer."

Her eyes welled up and she set her lip. All school year she'd been talking about the new girl, Cass. They had a relationship like lovers, always betraying one another and feeling offended, or desperately enamored, making each other cards and presents and promising undying fidelity.

We lived so far from town, we had to scramble for friends at school. Town kids walked out their front doors and found other children to play with. Out here, we had only each other. Lumi looked at those groups of kids with hunger in her eyes, and when she isolated one kid to play she nearly tackled them, laying her arms around their shoulders like an octopus, using her tentacles to keep them from running away.

"Play with other kids for a while."

She buried her head in the covers and made a dramatic little sob. "She's all I have."

* * *

My family still spoke, but I didn't hear them. Their words hit my ears, rising up and falling down, like birdsong you know and get used to: chickadee, junco, crow. If you paused to name them, of course you could, but usually they sat in the background to your more important thoughts. My family's conversations receded to scenery while the play was going, and I became an untethered mute.

A blue jay sounds like the unoiled squeak of a heavy chain, rubbing the metal bar overhead, back and forth, as a child swings. Except for the first sound, one syllable, plaintive as a word from a child to its mother—*why?* or *please?*—loud and repeated, but disconsolate, a child sure by now the mother won't respond.

"You want to be the little rag girl?" Miss X had asked me. "That's the part you want? Or a sack of potatoes? Are you a living, breathing sack of potatoes, child?"

Better that, I thought, than a body stared at by every boy, every man in town. Better that than a painted thing to be chased, ridiculed, and grabbed at. I thought of the exhausted, pinned-down look of the mama cat when the kittens came, her sore-looking teats, lying down to serve her children's needs, surrendering. *It's your destiny, girlie,* the whole world seemed to be saying. *All this land of surrender is yours. Come take your place, lie down. It's easy enough. And well, if not, it's still your only choice.*

I stood on the rag rug, our old life under my feet, woven together: soft denim of my father and brother, whisper floral of myself and my sister, even the hardy do-work of my mother's aprons and nightgowns turned to patterns of light and dark, sewn so tight it looked beautiful. Something to wipe your boots on as you entered the house, something to shake out every week, to bash against the bark of the oak tree, sending all the day's sand down to its roots.

Well, you'd have to believe in God, wouldn't you? If you were a woman? Got to be some reward for it, for the loyalty to husband and family, for the toil, and—as the old toothless miners say with their rolling Rs—*It sure as hell ain't here.*

But I was born with English in my mouth. Finn ways were the old ways. My mother could sweep her way to the horizons and never look up, never see anything. That was no way to live.

When I stood on the darkened stage it felt like a closed mouth, a French kiss already unwinding within it.

Everything that had ever happened had happened there: murder, betrayal, rape, love. Boredom, faeries, epics, rumbles. Floods and wars. Broken hearts. And though I stood there too, none of that was available to me. Mop girl. Tin can stacker. Broom pusher. Quiet mouse, no-voice mouse. Dreamer, to be pushed off the stage with the props. No use for a Finn girl, her mouth full of half-English. As if there were an American story already being told, a great Mississippi of a story filled with logs and boulders, sweet mud running south and cotton pushing north, and me no part of it. The Twain I'd read, *Huck Finn*, made me crazy with longing. That raft, what it meant, that you could pull on a pair of thick-kneed pants, rolled up at the ankles, and *go*, see all of it, stop anywhere. I would miss all of it. No chance to move, was there, never would be. Move to take care of another's floors. Move to be polite to yet another adult. Shut your mouth and do the work. Maybe someday you'll get a man and you can do the same for him, do the chores for him, hold down a small fort, look out the window as your hands roll out pie after pie. I didn't want to scrub. Didn't want to sweep. But on the stage, that floor of possibility, I couldn't do anything else. Could only stand like a lump and witness. Only my eyes moving, only my brain, trapped somehow within my Finnish head, making the connections, dreaming the dreams. Everyone could see. Everyone could laugh at the way I was all tied up, the way I'd agreed to tie myself up. No matter. Can't shape-shift if you won't. Stubborn, stubborn, stubborn girl. Won't take the cake that's offered you. Won't drink the cup from the well of clean cold water, because the well's not yours. You're only supposed to take what's yours.

10.
Socialista

The weather was turning inward, the wind and gray skies and cold pushing everyone back in their houses. Not yet the bright blue skies and sparkling snow of December or January which invited you out, but the rains that began before dawn and didn't quit for a week, the mold of leaves becoming slippery, losing their color to the ground. Animals growing nervous, the hunter's time just around the corner, the time of green shelter and easy food almost lost for another season.

Lumi began that October to write a story in pictures, her first unspooled not aloud but on paper. On the week-old *Socialista* painted over with glue and left to dry in the shed, then cut into small squares.

Her favorite paint was beet blood, deep pink like rabbit muscle freshly freed from its fur. She waited at my shoulder for the cooked beets to lose their skins, their bodies slabbed by my knife. Her tin painting cup, her old baby cup stamped with Humpty Dumpty before his fall, caught the beets' dark liquid as it ran from the oak board, which was already stained and colored by past vegetable and animal sacrifice.

Hawk quill snipped at an angle and a rabbit brush—fur married by wire to a barkless stick—were her tools. She made a slip of clay and water for her dark gray. Those grains were stubborn and stayed separate on the paper long after the water dried.

Lumi had learned to paint by painting Einar's house. Most people build in order, but not Einar. He included color, like lots of Finns, but he didn't do it with any apparent purpose or aim for harmony. Each board got its own color, *its own flavor*, he said, using the last of other people's cans, donated to the Finn Hall. He took them as they came, and painted as many boards as he could. Not together, which might have been easier and made more sense, but widely separated: a board near the roofline, a board near the door, equal numbers on each side but yards away from its closest neighbor. He let us children help, but it was still slow going. Most people used all their paint. And the Finn Hall had just as much need as Einar did for the donated cans. So he took what he could, let the rest of the cedar boards stand naked and fading to gray. I remember when I was small, he had painted only a few orange boards, a few robin's egg blue, but by now he'd covered the whole of the house: yellows and whites, reds and browns, and many shades of green. It looked like a drawing I'd seen of the witch's house in a Hans Christian Anderson book: the one Hansel and Gretel found their way to and, starving, began to devour. A candy house, a magic house, one that made you wonder just what kind of person lived inside.

Around ten o'clock that Sunday, Einar and Judy pulled in the drive. Isa had made one more run to Stearns County—"The last batch, I promise," he told Aiti—and for a share of the profits Judy would run it through her village in Mille Lacs.

The men stood in the shed for a while, staring at the jugs and eventually loading them up in Einar's car, but Judy and her nephews joined us in the house. I gave the boys Karl's old shirts to protect the clean ones they had on and they settled in at the table with Lumi. Edward, who was Lumi's age, swirled the beet juice into spirals with his pointer finger, adding salt to shatter the color into white stars, and his brother Hank, tall and quiet and just a few years older, left the messy things on the table, choosing instead to draw a penciled scene of a desert cowboy duel, prickly cacti leaning menacingly over the confrontation.

Karl, who had been my father's point man on the liquor until now, was surly about being cut out, so he stayed in with us and shunned the men outside, intermittently—and loudly—reading us sections from the *Aitkin Independent Age*, something we'd never seen in his hands before.

"Miner, 22, drowns while bathing," he said. "On the Whiteface River near Biwabik."

Aiti and the rest of us ignored him but Judy, being polite, said, "Oh? That's too bad." She had started in on the pie crusts while Aiti kneaded the ruisleipää, the rye bread she made from the same sour starter she'd carried in her pocket all the way from Finland.

We'd known Judy a while now, but I was still shy around her. Knowing she'd been in the pictures, that she'd been all the way to California, I thought maybe she pitied us a little, because who wouldn't? People stuck in one place like we were, doing nothing. I didn't know exactly why Judy came back home, though there must have been some love story involved. Her husband, who was from her band, volunteered for the Great War but never came back. We weren't supposed to bring him up around Judy, not least because Isa and Einar had been against the war on principle, on poor men dying for rich *kapitalisti* for no reason at all.

The men returned and found comfortable places to park themselves, each an early drink in hand.

Karl rustled the paper from his bed in the corner. "Drink Habit Cured!" he said. "Write to The Neal Institute, St. Paul."

Isa was in high spirits, clearly impressed with the new plans. "Men of vision find a way to serve the people, no matter what laws are on the books," he said. "The higher law of commerce and sharp wits! The entrepreneurial spirit! Rules are different out here. They moved somebody's house to the middle of the reservation, didn't they, to get the railroad through?"

Aiti said, "That was bad thing, Aarne," but he ignored her.

"If the money men can do it, why not us? You don't ask permission. You do what you have to, then play dumb and rake in the spoils. That's what men do. That's this free country."

"To the victor go the spoils," Einar agreed. "To the bold, the victory!"

Isa leaned forward in his chair. "People at the top have that luxury, to follow the law. But they make the laws, don't they? Down here in the dirt, we need other rules. Our own. Play by the law and you are a chump, under the boot of the powerful. And you know we all leave Europe for that." He leaned back, glared at the ceiling. "Exploit weakness. Take what you want. Don't admit you're wrong. That's how to get ahead."

"Combination Crocodile Wrench!" Karl said. "Grip and cut 5/16, 3/18, ½ inch. All for 1.75!"

Judy's gaze had stopped on the three kids painting. "You know, I've always wondered," she said, her voice dreamy and quiet, "why they let you keep your children."

Aiti looked up, obviously not sure she'd understood what had just been said.

"Only here a few years. Not using much English. Lots of you stirring up politics." Judy smiled. "You Red Finns."

Isa and Einar perked up a bit at that, but they were too worked up about their own train of thought to really hear her.

"They don't want us to have nothing," Isa said to Einar.

Judy laughed. "But I guess we're the dangerous ones." She told us about one time in California when she posed for an automobile advertisement. They wanted a group of barefooted Indians to chase a car, as if attacking it. In the background, later, the ad men drew a stagecoach being overtaken by tiny drawings of Indians. She held her thumb and pointer finger close together so we could see how small. "Little axes and everything." She mimed taking a chop, and the children laughed and ducked.

"Watch out, Einar!" Judy said. "We might chase you down sometime in Mille Lacs with our magical Indian speed."

"Einar, maybe you better find a young Finn girl," Isa said. "I hear they got a lot of them just waiting for a handsome bachelor like you."

Einar flushed to the roots of his beard and implored Isa without words to be silent.

"They give you the land they promised?" Aiti asked. Judy cut individual leaves from the crust trimmings, laid them in a wreath around the pie's edge.

"Nine years since Congress told Chief Migizi each family would get forty acres." She shook her head. "Still waiting."

"They don't know how stubborn you are," Einar said. "or they'd give up now."

Judy nodded. "We'll outlast them. They're blind and lazy."

"Blind and lazy," repeated the three children at the table. So focused and temporarily stilled, they looked like the three Fates creating, repairing, and judging the world.

"Fall Days are Picture Days," Karl said. "Bring us your film for best results."

I looked at him sharp for that, to see if somehow he knew where I'd been, but his face was hidden behind the pages, only his knees and stinky feet in view.

"Car Kills Child," Karl said. "*Imagine her racing down the hill in her wagon, her hair in the wind, and the tragedy as she reached the road...*"

"We want so many things we're not supposed to have," Isa said. "You just need some way to hide the money."

* * *

During rehearsals, when the chorus wasn't onstage, I found myself hiding more and more, up in the catwalk or slouched down in the high seats in the back.

> Dionysus. *Wait. How would you like to see their mountain seances?*
> Pentheus. *Very much. I'd pay a fortune in gold for that.*
> Dionysus. *Why, what gives you such a strong desire?*
> Pentheus. *Well...of course...I should be sorry to see them drunk, but...*
> Dionysus. *But, you would like to see them—sorrow and all?*
> Pentheus. *To be sure, if I could crouch quietly under the pines.*

In the dark, I could move with more ease. I got better at noticing which way the audience was looking, what had captured their attention, and could move freely in the blind space it created. When you didn't want to be seen, you needed to understand these things.

> Dionysus. *Come on out, you perverted man, so passionate for what is not for sight and acts that are not right—out,*

Jenny Robertson

Pentheus, I say, before the palace. Show me what you look like dressed up as a woman—a mad woman and a maenad—prying on your mother and her mob.

Otherwise you risked being caught in a spotlight when you weren't expecting it. I had nightmares about that, being exposed to ridicule, to the eyes of the crowd. Harsh light illuminated my inner thoughts, my secrets, my shames, and soon a town crier, played by the loudmouth of the group, would enter stage right, enumerating my sins for everyone's entertainment. Sometimes, if I was lucky, I'd disappear into the floorboards. Otherwise I stayed there forever and the laughter got louder, more cruel. I lost my clothes, piece by piece, each one given to an urchin in the audience who wore it around the stage, approximating my motions, which were ridiculous and deformed. The dreams ended with me naked, shaking and cold. Totally known, totally dismissed. A life reduced to nothing, a momentary diversion.

11.
The Last Words of Agave and Cadmus

Over the fall Karl hardened. He was always bluff armored, his presence calculated to strike fear or wary admiration, but now it seemed less a posture and more a change on the inside. Maybe he cared less, had gone stony in that place that used to be heartbeat vulnerable. His mouth showed it. Whether anyone was watching or not, it held a humorless straight line. His eyes looked through walls and people. Some movie, and not a hopeful one, played in front of them. The real, or at least what the rest of us thought of as real, was no longer of any importance to him. All of us inconsequential, beside the point.

He made new, older friends at the mine, went to town with them instead of riding home with Isa or Einar. Wouldn't see him till late in the evening, and then often stumbling and slurring. He'd fall into bed after eating the dinner Aiti saved for him. The evidence of his feast left spread all over the kitchen: dishes, fork and knife, tipped glass of milk.

But Aiti didn't coddle him. She swept him out of bed early in the morning, started folding up his bed with him in it. Sent him packing as if his bed was empty and no drunk son lay in it. Isa spoke up a few times, said he'd be a danger in the mine living that way, let down the others showing up tired, but Karl ignored him. Said *You wanted a working man. This is what you get.*

He left his traps to rust in the forest. Empty or full, they were no longer his concern. And yet he walked around, did his job, ate his food. It was frightening to watch. He was at the same time less alive and more physically imposing than I'd ever seen him.

And that was when the girls began to notice him. When he stopped caring. When he stopped smiling at them. When he hardened like ice and stone and looked through them. As though they were chasing a bear or a mythological half-man, half-beast. As though it were a competition, to see who could break the spell and make him a real boy again.

Karl never brought any girl home, but if we were in town together he got waves and winks from more than a couple. Girls older than him, ones living on their own in the boarding house or in their employers' homes. Young ones, my age. By ones and twos they watched him, moved closer to him. In groups they laughed and sought his attention. You could watch their eyes. Karl was magnetized, someone to try for. A prize. A catch.

He responded the same to all of them: a straight gaze, burning strong, that seemed to stop them in their tracks. His grim half-smile, half-sneer eventually made them blush and look away. He tipped his red-stained fingers to his cap as he passed, and you could see the girls, even the older ones, swoon right there on the sidewalk.

It was hard to hide my scorn for the girls and for Karl. He was no prince. No prize. I bet even Karl was scared that if they peeked under his surface, they'd find nothing of consequence.

I was with him in town on a bright day in November, the kind that makes you think maybe you'll skip winter's suffering this year, get to keep blue sky, calm breeze, and light jackets instead. After doing errands for our mother, I thought maybe we could head home, but Karl ran into some Barn Owls, friends who were still in high school.

"You don't miss it?" one asked. You could tell they looked up to Karl for some stupid reason. As if he hadn't been forced to go to work. As if he wasn't failing all his classes before that.

"I've got real plans," Karl said. "Can't waste my time with you kids anymore."

They play-punched his shoulder and teased him, but boys seemed to abide by the principle that the one who says he's tough is tough, and you tougher by proximity if you agree. They looked like a school of walleyes, sharp-toothed, muscley, wagging their tails lazily in the shallows before they'd strike.

"Maybe I'll drop by the rink this winter, show you a thing or two," Karl said.

Then there was a lot of excited talk: championship this, hat trick that. Best ever. Golden cup.

Who cares what any of you do, I thought. Pretending they were at the center of something, heartbeat of the town. And where is this town? Middle of nowhere, cut-over forest, sad sandy farms, potatoes and hay. Iron in the ground belongs to the moneybags, the ones who keep themselves clean. Throw foreigners in the drifts to make their fortunes. And call those foreigners names, sully their names, so they won't speak up too loud about how cold and damp, how dangerous it is, how low the pay. *Always more where you come from, Mongol. Don't think you're nobody special. You're lucky, you're lucky, you're lucky you got a job. Shut up and dig.*

Anger. Who knew what to do with it? If you were a girl, especially. Harsh words not allowed at home or at school, certainly not at the grocery. What to do with words of anger? Where to put them? Envy a man, who at least has people below him to empty his unhappiness on.

While Karl was showing off, I slipped away down the street to the photographer's alley. Since he'd taken our pictures I couldn't ditch my desire to see them. They would surely be developed by now. I wanted to see how we looked as other people in faraway places.

I ducked into the doorway and down the stairs without Karl seeing me and caught my breath at the landing as my eyes adjusted to the dim studio. The bear's hulking body came into focus first and soon after that the bulk of Mr. Swenson, who lounged in an overstuffed chair nearby.

"Well, if it isn't the Finnish flapper," he said.

How he knew I was a Finn I don't know, but I felt myself flush, as I did any time someone marked me as foreign. I wondered if my immigrant parents showed on my face or if my voice had given me away the last time I was here. I expected the photographer to get up, to be embarrassed to be caught at rest when he should have been working, but he stayed where he was.

"I came about the pictures," I said, self-conscious about each word as it left my mouth.

"Oh yes," he said. "I remember. So you'd like to take me up on my offer?"

I stared at him dumbly until he laughed. "I need girls to pose. Easy work. Whenever you have time. Ten dollars a sitting, cash."

I thought maybe I should run, but then he stood and retrieved the photographs from a flat wooden drawer.

"You still want to see?"

Of course I did.

He pulled out each picture with the tips of his fingers and spread them across a table. Celia and I as flappers, legs flashing. As grim cowboys. In front of a pyramid.

In sepia tones, all my imperfections blurred away. Whatever Miss X thought of me on the stage, in pictures I looked like an actress. In spite of myself I smiled at Mr. Swenson.

"Can I keep them?" I moved to take the photos as I asked, but he pulled them just out of reach.

"Don't want to ruin them with dirty fingers, do we?" He found a paper sleeve and handed them over.

"The cost?" I asked.

"For you, we'll start a tab," he said. "I can see you'll be good for it."

"Come back soon!" he called to my retreating back. I took the stairs two at a time, flew out of his shop, and ran straight into the brick wall of my brother's body.

"What the hell you doing?" He plucked the photos from my hand and held them up above my grasping hands. "Let's just see what we have here."

Karl's dirty hands pulling my pictures out in the open air had me immediately in tears. He laughed at that, and at Celia and I dressed as cowboys, but when he saw the one of us as flappers he looked like he wanted to bust through the photographer's door to strangle him.

"Don't," I said. "It's nothing. Just fun."

"Fun?" he said. "You know who does things like this? Whores, that's who."

If he had slapped me it wouldn't have stung more.

"What the hell you know about it?" I said. "That where your money goes?"

"Not something I have to pay for. Get it for free."

I snorted. "You never been with nobody."

"You want to see what kind of girls get their pictures taken? Look at these." He threw a deck of cards at me, the full set from which the girl and dappled horse had fallen. Inside were more girls in their natural state. Girls and grown women, fur and all. I only looked at three before I realized each image would mark me. I couldn't forget them if I tried. I stole back my pictures and threw the cards on the ground by his feet. Let him pick them up, kneel down to see all of them up close, he liked these captured girls so much.

I taught myself to drive Isa's car that day, left dust and gravel in my wake. Left Karl to walk home with his filthy women.

* * *

"One night only!" said the posters Miss X had pinned all over town. Most of us stayed after school the Friday of the performance. Hours till the audience filled with people, but what was the point of going home? The costumes were sewn, the paintings of the Acropolis fully dried. We had masks and snake-filled hair, fake blood, fake limbs, and a fake severed head. We maenads had bare, dirty feet and ragged brown wrappings meant to look like fawn skins. Everywhere were the sounds of flutes and tambourines, laughter and feigned intoxication. Everyone had given themselves over to the worship of the god of nature and wine.

Miss X let us run wild until call, an hour before the show, and we played tag between the dressing room and the wings, hollering on stage and dancing up and down the aisles of the theater trying not to get caught. At one point Marvelous, already dressed as hypnotized Agave, the homicidal mother of Pentheus, pulled me and the painter into the stage right curtain. It was funny at first, close and comforting, almost tent-like, two bodies pressed warm against me. For a minute all I heard was breath and giggles and fast hearts. But the fabric was so dense and heavy, and the light so completely blocked, I soon felt like running. *There's no air*, I said. *Hush, they'll find us*, Marvelous said. *We're fine*, the painter agreed. *Hold on a few more minutes*, but I couldn't bear it. I could be muffled here, never heard again. My whole body could be absorbed into these curtains, which suddenly seemed to hold some malevolent power. Other girls had surely disappeared in their embrace, thinking it a joke. A game. Why couldn't they feel it, the danger? I twisted to get out, but I'd picked the wrong rotation and my efforts tightened the fabric's grip on all three of us. Marvelous still laughed, but higher and louder now, as though she too were scared and asking for rescue in her own false-bravado way. The painter's breath was loud and ragged, and he murmured some comforting sounds I couldn't quite make out. In full panic I twisted the opposite way, a pike in a net suddenly aware of its own power, the great strength of a trapped animal, and the curtain unwound. I was dizzy by the time I found the opening, let in the cool stale air of the theater and ran free.

* * *

In a matter of hours, we'd reached the last scenes of *The Bacchae*. All those days and weeks of practice ended here: Marvelous as Agave, kneeling by the bier, saying, *My son, my son, whom these blind fingers tore apart and these callous eyes attacked, we know not what we do when we pride ourselves we know.* Kissing each part of his wrecked body.

I moved in formation with the women of the chorus and the mountain maenads. We schooled like fish waiting for the music—flute, tambourine, and drum—which would signal our exit.

The last words of Agave and Cadmus, just before the curtain closed and the audience's applause:

> Agave. *Goodbye to my house, goodbye to my city: I leave you for exile to flee from my bridal home. I leave you for misery.*
> Cadmus. *Many the forms of divine intervention: Many surprises are wrought by the gods. What was awaited was never created. What was ignored, God still found a way. Such is the story today.*

* * *

That night I dreamed I was hiding on the catwalk in our empty theater. All was still and dark until the lights came up to reveal Miss X in a silk robe, red dragons on a jade background. Underneath, she wore nothing and her skin, when she loosened the tie, was porcelain pale. Above shadowed thighs and round of belly, a small waist. From armpits and below, fiery hair. Small curves of breast and bright nipples. As she stood looking offstage, I wondered which part she was playing. Andromeda chained to the rock, maybe. Food for a monster, her own people willing to sacrifice her for the common good.

She pulled a long wooden pin from her hair and it descended in a cloud of golden-red around her face. I barely breathed, kept it low and shallow, so afraid my body would betray my position. She was the naked one, but I the one who felt ashamed, seeing her exposed where she shouldn't be.

From the wings stepped Dionysus. Miss X stood in place as he walked to within a few feet of her. They stayed like that for what seemed like great minutes, but was probably just a few breaths long. Their silence built a pull so strong it reached into the whole theater. It hit me as hard in my hidden perch as it did each seat, each entrance and exit, and the floorboards beneath their feet.

He looked like the Minotaur: hooves instead of feet, rooted by gnarled muscles to the floor. Thighs like hams, buttocks broad, back smooth as a trout's. His head was large and shaggy with curls. Low on his front, he carried a thick *kikkeli*.

He brought it and the rest of him to meet Miss X just as Aiti's voice up the stairs called me awake.

12.
Jaguars

The play was over just when I thought I might have found a new way to be. It was back to the store. Back to the family. I emerged from the theatre into a world from which all the orange leaves had fallen. Bare branches now and the threat of snow. Wind that swept people from the street and behind closed doors. We all smelled of woodfire now, and our skins began to itch and dry.

A November storm came through and left roads glistening with ice: all the vehicles, even the school bus, grounded. The mine covered too. A slip of soft glass over everything, too dangerous to send men moving over or under the ground.

Aiti had to be pushed out of the kitchen. She kept saying, *Just go, I come soon*, but we knew what that meant. She'd stay where she was, only heading out the door with her skates as she saw us returning, feigning disappointment as she said, *Oh, too bad. I come now to join you.* We had to take her with us right away and not give her the chance to change her mind.

"It's a once in a lifetime, Kata!" Isa said. "How often does the ice come before the snow?"

"I don't know, Aarne," she said, flour dusting her cheeks from the second kneading of the daily bread. "I don't pay so much attention to those things."

"Today you do," he said, and waltzed her a quick few steps. "Lumi, find your mother's skates."

So Miss X had thought I moved like a hunted sloth. It's because no one had waltzed me except Isa, when I was smaller than Lumi and could be lifted up and moved with no trouble. Aiti was lucky to have someone to waltz her just before she froze up and forgot how. Someone to break the ice before it got too thick and paralyzed everything.

* * *

The roads were too slick to walk on, but through the woods was fine. Each bootstep a crunch, brown-black leaves showing through. The ice not arresting anything, just covering it up, decoration on a lumpy cake. The old wintergreen stood out, with its small blood-red berries, some the color of strawberries. You wanted the red ones for the most concentrated flavor: cool and warm at the same time on your tongue when you bit through to the white insides. Lumi and I ate every one we could find.

Isa held the back of the line. *In case there are jaguars*, he said, and Lumi said *there are no JAGUARS in these woods* but laughed nervously anyway and scampered ahead so her big Isa would be the one eaten if the jaguars came. Karl led the pack. His superior tracking skills, he said, made him the natural choice. His woods. If you pushed him to it, he'd say they were. *What do you do with them*, he'd ask me. *What besides look?* Even though he'd given up his traps, he was still a young animal who'd marked his territory. Almost every tree held a notch or a symbol written in his own language, one we weren't meant to understand.

Our pond connected eventually to Foley Lake, the one by the mine. Just by a thread, a little gap through the forest, beaver-dammed at the junction, giving a thin stream of its water to the greater lake. But the pond near our house was an encircled world that seemed made just for us. It was protected from the wind by tamarack, birch, and pine, and too far from the river or the road to be worth logging. That morning chickadees called loud to warm themselves, puffing up their bodies within their shelter in the white pines.

In the summer, that pond edge was impassable: too mucky and deep with fine silt, a bed for clams and turtles, a shelter for minnows. You needed to dive shallow off the boards we'd laid soft over logs, a kind of partially-anchored raft built from scraps, and still the tops of the lilies and weeds brushed your belly. We'd kick hard from that shore till we reached the deeper water, unable to fight the feeling that we'd be pulled under by the green if we stayed where it could reach us. One leg cramp, one daydream, and the pond could take you.

But today the dry stalks and leaves of cattails whistled against one another, their fat brown sausage heads losing bits of white fluff. In between their stems and across the pond lay the smoothest ice I'd ever seen. Invisible, it was so clear. Just as scary, in its own way, as the summer weeds. Its promise: *I will hold you.* Do you believe such invitations? When your brother said, *Fall backwards, I'll catch you*? Who knows who waits to see you fall, to laugh at your trust.

We sat on a fallen tree, its bark high-glossed like a new Ford. Took off our mittens long enough to attach our skates and tighten them on our boots. I fixed Lumi's first, then my own. Lumi threw herself down at the edge, pressed her face to the ice. *I see turtles! I see frogs!* She moved out on the ice like a bear cub, her thick skirt padding her knees, her woolen tights showing her fat little calves.

"Wait, Lumi," Isa said. "Let the biggest ones go first. If I go in, you can save me."

"You won't go in," she said, her face stuck in a scowl. "Don't go."

"Don't you know, girlie, your father won all the races back in Finland? Fastest boy on skates in the whole country."

Karl made his underwater noise, doubt and challenge all at once, and they were off, the two fastest boys in America, to see who'd get the crown.

* * *

My father never looked so young to me as when he was skating. Usually he carried his worries on his face, his strength set against the work to come or dissipated by the work just finished. But his smile was wide and true, and his legs fast, on the ice.

Name a group of people most to be pitied: those who were never taught to skate. To set off with faith across a smooth clear surface. To push calf and thigh against a blade so thin it seemed to mock its stated purpose. Hold up full-grown people? Bear their weight? It couldn't be. Push off, feel those blades slip, but reach forward again and again until you find your rhythm. Take pleasure in the grate of blade against ice, in the mark you leave behind. Crisp shaved ice in your wake. Lines of power. Evidence of your journey.

You might think Aiti would be the slowest with her voluminous skirts, her buttoned-up bodice. But as a child she'd raced her siblings all the way to the island of Kotakari when it got cold enough to freeze the bay. She'd raced over sharks, she said. *You ever do that?* Skating was something even girls were allowed to do after chores, after church, during winter festivals. And she'd lost no edge. All of us, in our own way, were constrained by our roles on land. On ice clear as air, we were flyers.

Jenny Robertson

Funny how cold is not cold when you choose it. As we skated faster, the air slapped harder on our cheeks and our blood rose to meet it so we had hard skins, protection, as if we were animals meant for this weather, like the mink, like the feathered ones. As if we were given just what we needed to survive and could find joy in the heat inside us.

Isa took the lead for a crack-the-whip. First it was Aiti, then Karl, then me, then Lumi, who I held by one wool mitten, a string threaded through her coat sleeves so it couldn't go missing. Isa skated us in a long strong run first, across the pond. When we got so close to the edge I was sure he would wreck us, he stepped a hard dance to the left, his feet crossing over one another in tight stitches, and let us swing out. Lumi and I, at the end of the whip, skated over the edges of the reeds, surprising all the fishes and mud-buried frogs. We flew over the dry grasses captured in the freeze, heard their whispered music, their papery bodies shivering against one another.

I tried to hold onto Lumi, but a half-submerged log, its rough bark curving above the pond's surface, launched her out of my hands. She was briefly airborne and, though I wished silently that her knees would tuck up against her belly for protection, she stood straight as if she were able to walk on air just as easy as on frozen water. And when she landed—first on the long blades of her skates, then briefly balanced on their tips—I almost believed she might land without consequence.

But instead she became a seal, sliding on her belly across the ice until a wall of cattails stopped her. All of us converged on her padded starfish body, pulling her up, one person on each arm, to check her face, her head.

"I flew!" she said. "Did you see me?" No new gaps in her teeth, just the ones she'd had since summer. She'd be bruised on her knees and elbows, with an especially purple bloom on her chin, which she'd wear as badges of her flight.

* * *

Mummo died on the Sunday after Thanksgiving. Uncle Matti rang the party line. Emilie, the operator, connected us, then sat in silence and listened as my uncle gave my father the news. Mummo had set off for church on foot as usual, her round body packed tight in her mourning dress. Matti always offered to drive her to town but she said the Lord loved a pilgrim, that she pictured herself a child coming to Jesus's feet, called by the warmth of his smile. In the winter, she bowed to the snow and allowed herself to ride. And she forgave the storms that kept her housebound on the worst days, though not without mumbled curses and complaints. But this day was mild for December. We'd skated on the pond two weeks before, and the ice seemed firm and solid, as though it would last the year. But warm winds arrived from the south, one last burst of warmth before we were socked into the cold forever, and the inch of ice that had held our weight surrendered to the water without so much as a cry of protest. It just glistened and bobbed and let a wave overtake it. We'd gone down to the pond again with our skates in hopes of having it both ways: ice to skate and welcoming air to skate in. But it was gone, replaced by rows of standing whitecaps, all threatening movement where once there'd been a tamed and conquered stillness.

That morning as we walked back home disappointed, with our skates tied over our shoulders, their blades every third step poking us in the ribs, Mummo walked the county road. She liked to keep her polished shoes free from dirt and muck, so she stayed on the Portland cement and didn't move even when a car came along. She expected them to slow down and edge around her and they always did. It was a lovely walk from the farm into town, she said. You could see the whole village from on high, as the road twisted from the flat farmlands down into the river valley. She headed straight for the cross of Vor Frelsers Norsk Evangelisk Lutherske Menighed, Our Savior's Norwegian Evangelical Church, where the pastor gave the sermon in Norwegian, a language she didn't understand. She figured it didn't matter because she understood the Bible backwards and forwards and could tell what they were sermonizing about. Jesus would do the translating in her soul.

That day she traveled safely down the whole road, through the town's outskirts of grain silos and rough shops all the way to Main Street. She stood looking across the street to the open doors of the church, from which organ music—*How Great Thou Art*—was already playing. Observers said she adjusted her hatpins and smoothed down her skirt before she stepped from the sidewalk onto the street. She seemed certain that any traffic would, as they did on the county road, stop for her passage. But the poultry farmer with his cages of fat Christmas geese gained speed down the hill and turned the corner into town a little too fast. He had just looked back to see if he'd lost any cargo and didn't see Mummo until she flew up over his hood and shattered his windshield. He pressed the brakes long after it would do any good, small diamonds of glass sparkling all over his body and over that of the Finnish lady in black who lay on his lap. Her face when we saw it in the casket was covered with small cuts, and a great bruise stained its left side from the wisps of white pinned-up hair to the high lace collar of her dress. Her husband's hat was ruined in the crash so her head was naked. The part in her hair revealed a stripe of tender skin. It was the first time I'd been able to picture her as a child, her mouth pressed closed, it seemed, in sleep.

Lumi didn't want to be held up to see Mummo better. I knew she was afraid our grandmother would sit up and scare us, lecture us on the lengths she'd had to go to get us all in the church together. I might once have feared the same thing, but Mummo's injuries were so widespread and severe, I felt I now knew the meaning of unsurvivable. We'd often joked about Mummo's invincibility. Mummo versus influenza. Mummo versus smallpox. Mummo versus any number of English-speaking shop clerks—Mummo always the winner—but in a meeting between Mummo and a truck, our grandmother was the clear and mortal loser.

Mummo's corncob pipe, knocked from her purse along with a slim box of stove matches, lay on the swell of her belly, atop the table of her well-thumbed Bible. Her hands—much more delicate than they seemed to us when she lived—crossed one another just under her heart. Lumi contributed the black-eyed Susans which were Mummo's favorite flowers, silk and fake from the merchant's because it was too late for flowers from the field.

Uncle Matti and Isa had sent telegrams back to Finland notifying their older brother, a fisherman and father of six cousins we'd never met, of their mother's death. He sent back his own, the text the name of Mummo's favorite hymn: *Oi Jeesus yksin laupeus.*

* * *

"I don't like to say this. To accuse anybody in the family. But when you all were here last, some of Tall Boy's money disappeared. One hundred dollars. One hundred-dollar bill."

Uncle Matti kicked one boot against the leg of the table and cleared his throat. "We thought maybe it was someone here, but…"

"We had to promise some of the land," Aunt Hazel said. "Had to get a mortgage."

No one said it, but I knew everyone blamed Karl.

13.
Girls on Bicycles

They say one winter was so bad for so long all the people and the animals were snowed in place. They ate bark. They ate snow. They scraped the hides of the babies' diapers for any bit of nourishment. When people starved and died, they ate them. It sounds impossible, but people say it's true. Some things are that bad. And people don't know what they'll do till they're stuck someplace without choice.

We got snowed in at least once a year—days of blizzard, no way to dig out till it calmed—but usually those were good days. No work, no school, only a fire cooking in the stove, enough wood piled just outside the door, and enough dry inside to keep us toasty. Watching the wind blowing sideways, Isa was proud of his tight joinery, no gaps in this house to let in the cold. Man bigger than storm, for once.

So much coffee—a pot on the stove all day and into the night—hot cup and all the newspapers, books and catalogs, soft sweet pipe.

"I'm a man of leisure!" Isa said on one of those days in January, poking at the advertisement for the young executive in the *Pioneer Press*, his feet up on a padded stool, surrounded by luxury. "Look, Kata! Who is richer than we?"

Though he was full of pie, which usually knocked him into an unplanned nap, Einar shifted in his seat and cleared his throat so much Isa had to quit reading the paper to ask him what was wrong.

"I'm thinking maybe I'm done there at the Milford."

I'm not sure we'd ever heard a more shocking statement from Einar. He wasn't a man who seemed to have a lot of other options. While everyone else had been drinking coffee, Einar and Karl had sipped on their whiskey flasks, so maybe that explained it. Isa must have doubted his sincerity, because he didn't say a word.

"My coat's about ripped to shreds from that cage. They don't even give us no protection."

Isa nodded.

Einar, encouraged, continued.

"And you know they got us digging too far under the lake." He paused. "They found sand only five foot over the rock, above that new drift."

"Aarne?" Aiti worried too much, Isa said, so he didn't tell her about things that were going wrong.

"Kata, it's fine. Those big shots gonna get every bit of iron manganese they can, even if we gotta swim to dig it."

That joke didn't go over well, so Isa tried another tack.

"It's nice down there, you know, where the wind can't reach. Hell of a lot warmer than up here, especially if you dig awhile. You got the wrong idea, staying up when you could be down." He hit Aiti's bottom as she walked by his chair. "You should come down and see."

"What I do there, eh? Wear some hardhat? Smoke the cigarettes? Maybe dynamite?"

"You would be a good looking miner," Isa admitted. "Look good in mining clothes. Tough enough woman. Have to close your ears, though. Boys tell a lotta jokes."

"I heard your jokes. Dirty boys don't scare me."

Karl looked peeved by the idea of Einar leaving. Maybe it gave him the idea he could leave sometime too. "You know they got a big deal going on in Karelia," he said. "Lots of young Suomi going back home." There was land, he said, just waiting for strong men like him. Adventurers. Pioneers.

"Sure, you're a real Jack London type!" Einar said.

Karl kept on, earnest as Isa now. You could go to Karelia, be part of something bigger, he said. The forests ten times as vast, the trees three men wide, the lakes deep and cold, just right for the workers who'd bathe in them after a long day logging and farming, building a fair and just world for the common people.

"*Jo.* That's the dream," Isa said. "That's the same dream they sold us, boy. A worker's paradise."

"This isn't *kapitalisti*," Karl said. "This is a whole new system. *Socialisti.*" Karl pointed at the paper in Isa's lap as if to say *Are your principles, in the end, only words? Only things to read and never to do anything about?*

Karl was all muscle in those days, even where there should have been brains. What to do with whole countries filled with boys like that? Someone's gonna sell them a project, you don't give them one that's tempting enough.

When Isa didn't respond, Karl stood up and dropped his playing cards in Einar's lap. He put his finger to his lips and raised his eyebrows toward Aiti, who was busy doing other things.

After a few minutes of perusal, Einar couldn't hold in his enthusiasm for what he was seeing. "I am just telling you!" His voice was whiskey-raised and passionate now, though there was no need for him to shout to be heard. "If she wanted to do dirty things with me I would *let* her."

"What kinds of dirty things?" Karl's mouth hung open in a wolfie grin. I expected to see him drool. "See, Sadie? This is what people say about girls who show their skins."

"You, Karl. Shut up," Aiti said. "Your sister don't need to hear that. I know what you got there, Einar. Put those away."

"You think she's so pure. Know nothing," Karl mumbled. Then, louder, "Like I don't already know what's what. I *work* in the *mine*."

Aiti addressed the stove. "He such a big man. Can tell him nothing. Already knows. I should ask him, what I should do next. My son would know. Why I think or say anything, when I got such smart son? *Eilisen teeren poikaot!*" Not son of yesterday's grouse, she said.

"Don't expect me at the mine either," Karl said.

At first Isa ignored him, but when Karl didn't take it back he stood up too, and threw his paper on the ground. "What should I tell the boss, eh? My son so stinking drunk, such a *kalsarikanni*, he can't show up for work?"

Karl didn't answer.

"What you going to do, Karl? I just don't know. It's like you want to shit on everything."

"You want me to be like you, break down into nothing, not even a man anymore. You'll die down there, an old man. I ain't gonna do that."

"Ya, ya, you'll do so much. I can see that. Bright future you got there. Anybody would say."

"I can sell whiskey."

"You drink whiskey," Isa said. "Where's the money, Karl? All this money you make selling. It's in your pockets now? How much you got? Enough to buy a big *kaari*? Enough for a house?"

"Takes time."

"Takes brains. You ain't got those."

"Takes brains to do something new. Takes guts to stay in the open air."

"Should we ask your teachers? Kata, where the boy's report cards? From all the years."

He got up from his chair, pulled out drawers from the dresser where Aiti kept all the important papers, our childhood drawings, letters from Finland. "They in here?"

She moved to stop him. "Aarne, let me. You're going to ruin everything."

"Ruin? I'm not the one doing that. You're looking the wrong direction." He pointed one red finger toward my brother. "This the one bringing shame and ruin on the family. He is the one. Never thought I'd see the day when my own son would steal money from my brother, from his own family. Not work. Drink all day. Not gonna let that happen. It ends now. You go to work. *Joko teet tai itket ja teet*," he said. *Either you'll do it, or you'll cry and you'll do it.*

Karl turned iron-red, grabbed his jacket from the peg on the wall, and his snowshoes. "Right. I am the thief."

"Karl, it's cold," Aiti said. "Where you going?"

"I don't stay where I'm not wanted, Aiti. I'm so bad, find another son, maybe. Pick one up on the side of the road. Someone who'll shut up and stay underground, like Isa wants. Maybe dig in the yard, you'll find one."

* * *

As soon as the blizzard broke I put on skis and cut through the field where we collected chokecherries at the end of summer. It was filled with small trees, their thin branches extended to the sun. There were no pines to suffocate the ground with needles, to intercept and steal the light. Just stillness and the tracks, sometimes clear and well-grooved, sometimes filled in with winddrift snow. The quiet of a still winter day, low sun steady. The sound of my own heart, my own breath so loud in my ears that the chickadees' regular conversation and the crows' protests and the squirrels' brief appearances to talk and warm their fur felt filtered and far away.

Anything could sneak up when you were in that state, pumping your arms and legs in rhythm, sweating into the woolens you'd needed as protection when you started out but had to stop to remove. Every few minutes another layer gone. And your heat keeps stoking higher even after the sun completes its brief tour above the trees and falls again into their top branches. You don't notice at first that the source of your warmth is leaving, and decide too late, only after a breeze begins and chills the sweat on your neck, that you maybe shouldn't have let yourself get so sweaty or moved so fast. That you should have stayed steady and slow and peaceful, your clothes dry, your skin dry, if you wanted to arrive in one piece.

* * *

Mummo always said the devil was real, but where is hell, anyway? Men have been digging deep in the earth a long time and all they find is iron and water. No fire anywhere. Or maybe hell is dark earth and water and no way to get yourself to the surface. I could buy that. A miner's hell, anyway. The devil you know, with no escape from it. Or hell might have been the secret back room of Mr. Swenson's shop. When I skied into town and showed up at his door, he didn't say a word, just swept me through the black curtains into that room, which was warm with its own potbelly stove cooking away.

I stood in front of the stove's red face to warm my wet hands, my snowy pants and socks, and perused the wall behind it. Every inch was covered in postcards and photographs, barely a gap between them. Girls on bicycles, crashed, their skirts raised to show they'd forgotten their underwear. Men standing behind girls on bicycles, their hands cupping the girls' asses to steady them. A girl kneeling at the front of a broken-down car, checking its undercarriage, while an unseen observer checks hers. Girls on park benches, legs raised to expose garters and stockings and fat white thighs. Girls together, their hands and mouths busy with each other's breasts. Girl maids up on ladders, the man of the house bending to spy through a peephole. That man emerging from behind screens to embrace the maid where she perches on the third rung. Maid turning to smile at the man, feather duster forgotten for now. Indian maidens, shy peek of a breast from deerskin cover. Middle Eastern women, half-dressed around a carpet feast. Three lynched men, in front of the courthouse in Duluth in 1920. Proud men standing around the bodies. Thirty-eight Dakota men hanged in Mankato. Proud people—men, women, and children—standing around them. Next to them picture after picture of giant fish and the men that caught them. Alien mouths gaping in the dry human air. Speckles and stripes, fins and teeth. The men smiled and held still in their best poses.

* * *

"That's more like it. Chin up, so I can see your face. Got a strong one." Swenson traced my cheekbone up toward my ear, brushed a stray hair from my forehead. Touched that finger to his tongue. "Mongol salt," he said. "You're not so red up close. More yellow, maybe. I always wondered, did they call you that because of your skin or your politics, or was it some convergence of the two? I hear you all drink and fight, live in squalor. Do you live in squalor, young Mongol? Would you know the difference if you were plucked out and put in a clean house? Or would you soil it immediately so you felt more at home?

"It's not your fault, of course. No one chooses who they're born to." He wagged his finger. "But that doesn't mean there's any escape." He sat up, appraised me again, linked his hands around my head. "They've studied it, you know. It's all in the shape of your skull. How much brain you were given and of what quality. Europeans are the pinnacle of evolution. We evolved bigger brains while your relatives were still squabbling in caves, digging in the dirt with bones. Are those tears? It's too late to do anything about it now, sweet girl, so don't feel sorry for yourself. You're still good for a few things. Better, even, for a few things."

* * *

Picture Karl swooping in then, three sheets to the wind, the bantam in him fully lit from within, his talons sharp, iron-fisted. No matter that a touch at the right point of his shoulder would've knocked him over. No matter that soon he'd be emptying his guts of shine. There's been no greater fighter born than the Finn Rocket, in Minnesota or across the sea. And liquor only added fuel to his anger, at least for the space of one righteous fight.

Swenson's temple caved in on the first punch—you could hear it go—the muffled reception of arriving knuckles, a giving in on the soft edges, less defended than the orbital skull around the eye. His large brain met by Mongol brutality. I was sure that in those few seconds between the punch and the fizzle of light and sound, the photographer thought about that, the great waste. How brute strength had beaten superior mind, robbing evolution of its brilliant arc toward perfection.

14.
Under

I don't remember anything. There once was, then there wasn't, a mine. There once were rooms and hallways, darkdamp and sulfur, under the ground. Hard rock, machinery, bad air and fresh. Men. There once were men under the ground. Fathers. Sons. Bachelors. Married. The vigor of a dozen nations, men who'd survived an Atlantic crossing, cobbled houses from the woods, raised children to speak a language they still tripped over. There once was a world under our feet. We felt them moving there wherever we went. On the way to school, on Main Street. Even in the woods. Even swimming. They were always digging, always exploding, always sweating, laughing, and swearing. Always talking with their hands. Always smoking. Always counting the hours and the weight of the ore. Always hoping the lantern would stay lit. Always trusting the timbers to protect them from the weight of all of us, the weight of the whole town, the whole world, above them. This isn't new. Men have been digging our dinners out of the earth for centuries. Other men, still clean, tallying numbers on the surface, have always hired men to do that digging. This isn't new. None of this is new.

* * *

Under the water ...
... can they hear anything?

Jenny Robertson

Did you hear about the Jones boy?
Speak Italy?
I'll patch you through.
We don't know anything yet.
Hold a minute please . . .
Yes, sir, right away.
They'll be there in five minutes. They'll be bringing up the cage. He said he was the last one there. Someone was behind him but he must have let go.
The water came fast. The air changed and it got dark and then it was cold dark water and they ran as fast as they could but some guys they didn't make it . . .
Hold.
Is Joe down there today?
I don't know.
Yes? Hold please. I'll connect you.
Hold for the Foreman. Yes ma'am.
Pioneer Press? Yes sir. No sir. I can't give you any information on that sir. I've got to clear the line for rescuers and families. Thirty-eight missing.
No. First shift. Forty minutes before second shift. No. No. I'm sure.
The headphones hot circles, ears ringing like a head cold, the repetition. Eighteen years old and a brother below and *No mother I can't talk now no I haven't heard anything. Hold. Hold. Yes, I'll call you. No, don't tell me if you find out till after my shift. No. Hold please.*

* * *

The siren wailed for hours, until they disconnected it at the surface. Somewhere below, its cord remained wrapped around the man who sounded it.

* * *

They closed it down, after, all the roads into the mine. No men swinging pails as they walked to work. No men piling out of cars together. No men making jokes in the changing room or in the cage as they readied to descend. No men singing hallelujah in every language as they rose to meet the air.

Well, that's what should have happened. They should have closed it after that, treated it like the sacred cemetery that it was. But they said the loved ones wanted the bodies pulled out, counted, so they could be buried on land.

"What difference?" Aiti said. "Buried. God in heaven, BURIED."

I pictured them asleep down there while they waited for the pumps to do their slow work, moving the lake like that from the drifts to the topside, filling another pond. Imagine what the fish made of that, all that swamp water fallen through caves, red with iron, filled with screams, pumped back into their placid homes where before only blue sky was reflected on its surface of skimmer bugs and resting dragonflies. I pictured it as a pollution, a curse, but what else were they going to do?

Aiti wished they'd left them there, buried, as she said. Tucked into bed is how I pictured it. In a watery bed, like in the sea shanties Uncle Matti liked to sing. Some sailor always ending up that way, thrown overboard to sleep forever. But our boys, our men, floated under in darkness, their torchlights extinguished by the rush of air that came first: wind, then darkness, then water. That sequence replaying in our minds, always, but especially in the moments before we fell asleep. No matter how tired we were, when we lay down in bed and the lights went out we saw what they saw, we felt what they felt, our bodies tensed as we realized, just as they did, that what we heard was water. That it filled the tunnels. That only the few closest to the cage, far away from us, our brothers, would have any chance at all. And we'd remember the flimsy ladder, rungs missing, one man at a time. And the shaft that was always blocked with timber. And then the cold of it, February water, just barely not ice, filled with loam and peat, dirt and root, centuries of rot and layered leaves, all that water interfering between their feet and the floor, washing their boots, hoisting their legs, wrapping round their torsos, filling their throats, combing their hair, removing their hats as though this were a fine cathedral, a solemn occasion. Baptism is too easy a metaphor. Trade air for dirt and water. Trade the warmth of living body for the cold preservation of death. Replace their sweat with lake water. Remember summer days, long jumps off docks, shouts of *Holy Jesus, it's cold*, resounding laughter and concussion of splash as one after the other, just off shift, peeled the work off themselves and entered innocent as born babes, careful not to touch the weedy bottom, not to disturb the weight of muck that fell soft and giving, maybe for miles, beneath them.

* * *

Maybe they'd holed up in a new drift above the waterline. Maybe there was a drift, a tunnel arm, that had angled upward just enough. Maybe some bored miner had planned a new ladder, a ladder to nowhere, and their men had climbed it and were waiting, cold and in the dark but safe, and were telling jokes right now, sharing the last of their lunches, tapping out Morse code on a steel pipe that soon a mine investigator, or a small child, would hear topside: *I heard a noise*, they'd say later. *I almost didn't stop. But I had this feeling, and I stopped and put my ear to the ground and I heard* it: *H.E.L.P. The same code we learned in Boy Scouts, the same code they used in the war.* And then the tale of running back breathless, telling a group of adults and the adults shaking their heads, sorrowful: *it couldn't be.* But following the child anyway, because he wouldn't be silent. One man, to humor him, bends his grown body to the soil, listens without hope before exclaiming: *Everyone! Everyone, be quiet! By George, he's right. Oh my god, he's right! They're alive!*

And then the rustle of maps and the shouting of orders, the little Scout patted and scooped up and embraced— *Good man!*—as they traced the drift from the spot, marked out the paces, compared it to the master plan. *By Jove, let's get them out!* And the tense race to—carefully, carefully— sink a new hole, close enough to get to the men, but not enough to collapse their air pocket. Hoping against hope that they wouldn't draw water from the main shaft into their last refuge.

I replayed it in my mind, knowing somehow that the whole town shared the same dream. That if we put our minds to it at the same time, enough times, we could drill to the men, exactly where they waited. We could let the miracle happen. It only required a collective act of will.

* * *

Aiti in black was a different Aiti. Could have dressed her in sackcloth, though, she wouldn't have cared. Sure, she still moved through the routines of the house. You couldn't stop her. Every surface shone. No dust could resist her. She baked, though neighbors brought pie. Eight on the windowsill at once, all in a row. The most beautiful smells: cinnamon, cloves, fall apple, pumpkin. Rolls in elaborate tortured shapes. Great stews. Monstrous roasts. The largest pot of the largest potatoes, whipped with great lumps of butter. It was a production line to rival Ford. The greatest feast we'd ever had. Neighbor ladies came in expecting to see her prone, lacking all will and ability to move, children mopping her forehead. They were ready to take over her kitchen, fill it with their busy hands, their best recipes, but Aiti would not cede the floor. She stayed on her feet, in the dead center of the kitchen, from dawn to dusk. She acknowledged the women with nods and thank yous, took their offerings and placed them with all the others, then she swept them to the table where she filled their coffees, set plates before them, a carving ham, with knife (*You kutti. Won't bite you.*), a pie server loaded up with the first piece of their own pie. Some ladies tried to leave. They'd intended only to come, to say a few words, maybe to take some of the washing, do some dishes, then go, holding their purses like holy books before them. But Aiti treated them as if they were customers in her busy restaurant. She did not entertain. She was too busy cooking, checking the top of a pie with one heat-tempered finger, moving pans around in the oven, whisking a gravy, wiping sweat from her brow with the corner of her apron, then facing the tasks before her with renewed vigor.

Only when she saw Judy out in the yard, standing with her hands clasped before her as if they held a lifeline, did she lay down her work. She fell out the door and into Judy's arms and they walked away like that into the woods and didn't come back until all the visitors had left.

After

They let all the prisoners out of the jail after the accident. Needed every man they could get. So Karl never paid for what he did. I guess they figured he'd suffered enough losing a father. And from guilt, because by all rights he should have been down there too. A few years after that, when he sobered up, he married one of the telephone operators. Emilie, the one who told us about Mummo's passing and who lost one of her own brothers in the mine. Well, who didn't lose? Eighty children had no father that day.

The two of them stayed in town for a while after the wedding. We got to meet their first child, a girl they called Stella. But they lit out for Karelia when Emilie was pregnant with their second child. It was a boy. Daniel, it said in the letter. They were happy at first, caught up in the revolutionary spirit of the new socialist community. But the letters grew grim, and less frequent, as things changed. The Soviets moved the Finns into work camps. Food and heat were hard to come by. The letters stopped in 1936, during the height of the crackdown on "bourgeois nationalists," which included the returned and invited Finns.

* * *

Judy lived in Einar's house for a few years, until Congress finally made good on its promise to give her people land. Of course they only got five acres, not forty like they'd been promised, but Judy said she hadn't expected any better. She said I could have Einar's house after that, pay her on an installment plan, so I moved in. Its wild colors suited me, though it never lost its faint scent of Finn bachelor. You might not believe it, but eventually I took over the job of theatre director at the school, and in town too. We put on musicals, mostly. People wanted singing and dancing, especially when things got rough. The usual romances. The tragedies. But sometimes Miss X would come through town with her traveling troupe and we'd put on the new plays, the wild ones. Make a scene in the newspapers. So I guess the Finn mouse found her voice, after everything. Though I still stayed in the shadows and watched most of the time. It was more natural to me. Let the Marvelous ones hold the stage and wear the costumes. They can have it.

* * *

I give myself some credit for Lumi's escape. At fifteen, three years into the Great Depression—enough time to tell there'd be no recovery, no savior coming for any of us—she chopped her hair tight to her head, except for one shock of blonde bangs hanging over one eyebrow, wrapped her breasts with foot-wide linen, and traded her skirts for trousers. She jumped the train as it left for the west. Passed as a boy all the way to Seattle, then Portland, and all the way to San Francisco. Aiti got postcards from all the cities. She kept them in her purse to share with everyone, made a big show of disparaging her wayward daughter—*disobedient, shocking, breaking the rules*—but everyone knew that deep down she was thrilled. That she was bragging about the one who got away. Lumi became a girl again—a woman, I guess—when she reached the coast, but she kept the pants. She started selling smoked fish from a little open-air shack on the beach, and I think she did well there. One thing our parents taught us was to work, so it wasn't too much of a surprise.

Or maybe she got the idea from Judy. Probably. Her big sister never was much of an actress.

Acknowledgments

Grateful acknowledgment is made to the publications in which the following stories first appeared:

"Sex-O-Rama, 1993" in *Gulf Stream Literary Magazine* (fiction winner)
"Lifted" in *SLAB*
"The Triumphant Return of Maggie Pancake" in *Hypertext Magazine*
"Ground Truth" in *South Carolina Review*
"The Improviser" in *Flyway-Journal of Writing and Environment*
"Green Skins" in *The Best of Cutthroat* (awarded Rick DeMarinis Short Story Competition 2nd Prize by judge Stuart Dybek).

Many thanks to my mentors at Pacific University: Craig Lesley, Pam Houston, Bonnie Jo Campbell, and Jack Driscoll. As well as Claire Davis, who reminded me to "smell the corn." Thanks to my mentors at the University of Louisiana at Lafayette: John McNally, Joanna Davis-McElligatt, Dayana Stetco, Matthew Griffin, and Mary Ann Wilson. For their encouragement and feedback, thanks to Britton Andrews, Alexandra Lytton Regalado, Daniel Bohnhorst, Kierstin Bridger, Traci Moore, Lisa Ortiz, Andrew Watson, Daniel Altenburg, Josie Scanlan, Leigh Camacho Rourks, Rebecca Hazelwood, Jen Sperry-Steinorth, and Dan Calhoun. Many thanks to Writing by Writers, Bear River Writers' Conference, and the Lillian E. Smith Center at

Piedmont College for fellowships and residencies during the writing of this book. I also want to thank my students at the University of Louisiana at Lafayette, Ellipsis Writing, Interlochen Arts Camp, and Front Street Writers. Thanks to Amy, Kris, Erika, Janna, and Anee for years of memories and ongoing friendship. Thanks to the Nagel family and, always, to Kia, whose light and laughter are woven through everything I write.

This book has benefitted greatly from historical research and archives: from local newspapers to interviews with Finnish-American immigrants to journal articles concerning 1920s politics, Ojibwe history, mining, labor relations, and countless other topics. Many thanks to the historians, writers, and academics who make their findings accessible to the public and to writers like me.

Thanks to Dr. Ross Tangedal and the fearless, talented crew at Cornerstone Press, including Brett Hill, Maria Scherer, and Julia Kaufman. Many thanks to my parents and my big little brother for a childhood filled with nature, music, and books. Thanks always to Ian and Ethan for going on this wild ride with me. You are my heart.

JENNY ROBERTSON is a fiction writer and poet from Minnesota and Michigan currently living in Wisconsin. Her chapbook of short fiction, *Hard Winter, First Thaw*, was published in 2009. Her fiction has appeared in *Hypertext Magazine*, *South Carolina Review*, *Cutthroat*, and *SLAB*, and she has been awarded the William J. Shaw Prize for Poetry. She has served as Writer-in-Residence for Front Street Writers and as Creative Writing Instructor at Interlochen Arts Camp, and has been awarded a residency at the Lillian E. Smith Center as well as fellowships to the Writing by Writers and Bear River Writers Conferences. She holds an MFA in fiction from Pacific University and a PhD in English from the University of Louisiana at Lafayette.

Printed in the USA
CPSIA information can be obtained
at www.ICGtesting.com
LVHW041326051023
760079LV00007B/1082